SWIMMING

SWIMMING

KARL LUNTTA

excelsior editions

State University of New York Press
Albany, New York

Published by State University of New York Press, Albany

Excelsior Editions is an imprint of State University of New York Press

For information, contact State University of New York Press, Albany, NY
www.sunypress.edu

Production, Jenn Bennett
Marketing, Kate R. Seburyamo

Library of Congress Cataloging-in-Publication Data
Luntta, Karl, 1955-
    [Short stories. Selections]
    Swimming / Karl Luntta.
        pages ; cm. — (Excelsior editions)
    ISBN 978-1-4384-5872-4 (softcover : acid-free paper)
    ISBN 978-1-4384-5874-8 (ebook)
    I. Title.
    PS3612.U58A6 2015
    813'.6—dc23
                                                    2014049312

10 9 8 7 6 5 4 3 2 1

This book is for Phyllis,
and for Nikki, and Kaarlo, and Jack

CONTENTS

Acknowledgments / ix

A Virgin Twice / 1

Swimming / 27

Jeff Call Beth / 47

Cold on Ice / 69

His Sanitary Bed / 87

Blue Jays / 105

Dancing / 133

At Times like This / 149

ACKNOWLEDGMENTS

"A Virgin Twice" was first published in *International Quarterly*, collected in *Living on the Edge*

"Swimming" published in *Toronto Review*

"Jeff Call Beth" published in *Talking River Review*

"At Times like This" H. E. Francis Literary Competition, University of Alabama-Huntsville

"Cold on Ice" published in *Northeast Corridor*

"His Sanitary Bed" published in *Buffalo Spree*

"Blue Jays" unpublished

"Dancing" published in *Buffalo Spree*

A VIRGIN TWICE

In the early evening, as the jacaranda trees opened their blossoms to do battle with the stale heat of the day, a small boy appeared on Kevin's stoop. It was less than four hours since the incident with Mdongo.

"*Ko ko,*" the boy said. "Sah, sah!"

Kevin came to the door and the boy was on one knee, his eyes averted.

"You don't have to do that," Kevin said. "It's not necessary." He realized it was foolish of him to say it, yet he always felt compelled to say it. Sometimes he did, and sometimes he didn't.

"Yes, sah," the boy said, but kept his eyes and knee to the ground. His head was powdered with fine dust and his back rose and fell rapidly.

"Yes?" Kevin said.

"I am sent by Kgosi Lesetedi. He is calling you," the boy said, breathlessly.

"Yes, of course he is," Kevin said, still feeling numb about the whole thing. "There you go."

"Go to where, sah?"

"Not you. I meant—it's an expression."

"Yes, sah."

"Okay, you can tell the kgosi that I'm coming."

"Will I wait for you?"

"No, I need to wash first. Just tell him I'm coming."

"Yes, sah," the boy said. He remained on the ground, waiting to be dismissed.

"What is your name?" Kevin asked.

"Mosimanegape, sah," the boy said.

In his mind, Kevin flipped the pages of his language manual. "What does it mean?"

"It means 'Another boy,' sah."

Kevin looked down at Mosimanegape. His back was covered, in a manner, by a brown schoolboy's shirt, tattered at the collar and threadbare at the broad of the shoulders. "You're not one of my students, are you?" Kevin said.

"No, sah. But next year I will have you for maths."

"Looking forward to it?"

"Yes, sah," the boy said.

Kevin nodded, but the boy didn't see it. "Mosimanegape, just for my information, when would a boy like you be allowed to stand and talk to an adult?"

The boy kept his eyes to the ground while he thought about it. "I have never thought about it, sah," he said, finally.

"Never? Let's say that you were sixty years old, would you look me in the eye when you talk to me?"

The boy giggled, embarrassed by the thought. "No, sah," he said.

2

"Why is that?"

"Because when I am sixty, you will be dead."

"Well," Kevin said. "You know your maths, at any rate."

"Yes, sah."

"Just tell him I will be there soon," Kevin said. He hesitated for a moment. "Okay, you may go."

The boy stood up and backed away, his eyes still to the ground. When he reached the main gate, he turned, waved, and sprinted off.

Kevin walked back to his tiny kitchen and picked up his yet untouched gin and tonic. He decided against it, and placed it back on the shelf next to some tin plates and cups. He took a brown paper bag and placed it over the drink, to shield it from bees.

He went into his bedroom to dress for the occasion. He was, after all, meeting with the chief of the entire village. He decided shorts would be too informal, and a T-shirt would be close to disrespectful. He settled on clean khaki trousers and an ugly African-print safari shirt, one that he'd bought early on at Patel's Haberdashery in Gaborone. He hadn't even liked the shirt when he saw it, but bought it anyway, reasoning that it was the type of shirt that would bring him closer to the people. Within days he realized he hadn't seen a single African man wearing the same type of shirt. They were all whites—British expatriates, development workers, people like him. When he checked the label and saw it had been manufactured in Taiwan, he considered throwing it away. Still, he was sentimental about it, and held onto the shirt. It was a landmark shirt.

Kevin stripped down to his waist and rubbed the bruise on his shoulder where Mdongo, who was both the headmaster of the school and a madman, had bitten him. Mdongo had not, in the words of the medical manual Kevin used to treat himself, "impugned the integrity of the skin." Still, he was grateful for delivery from tetanus or God knows what. It was God knows what that could kill a person out here. The nearest hospital was half a day's ride.

He examined the scraped knuckles of his right hand, and doused them again with hydrogen peroxide. The liquid bubbled and fizzed, raising a stinging strawberry parfait on his knuckles. He vaguely recalled that a student had snatched Mdongo's tooth from the ground after it had left the headmaster's mouth and arced in slow motion, tumbling through the air before it hit the dust. The student no doubt still had the tooth, and would later use it as a fetish, insurance against bad grades and capricious discipline.

Five minutes later Kevin was dressed and out of the house. The jacaranda mingled with the acrid smoke of acacia-wood cooking fires, as women prepared dinners throughout the village. As he walked, small children darted in and out of the compounds, chewing on a chicken leg here, pushing a toy truck constructed from soft drink tins there. Some stopped and stared when they saw him, calling out, "Mista Keveen!" But when he looked back at them, they averted their eyes and giggled.

Miss Ndlovu's compound was subdued. A few children chased goats from the plastic water basins, but most of her people would be at the kgosi's place, waiting to hear the story. Miss Ndlovu was, of course, well on her way to the hospital, if not already there.

Peter Zimunya's rondavel was also dark and quiet. Kevin was sure his friend was already sitting with Kgosi

Lesetedi, exchanging pleasantries about the weather and lack of rain, or about the status of cattle diseases this year.

Kevin approached the entrance to the school and saw a small crowd gathered around the staffroom. Some simply peered, awestruck, through the burglar-barred windows. Others talked excitedly and pointed at Kevin as he walked by. "Jesus," he said to himself. "What now?"

The crowd was at a distance, so he tried to wave them off. Some waved back, good-naturedly, misinterpreting his gesture. In the crowd he spotted Rose, a woman he'd been sleeping with. He would have preferred to say that he was having a relationship, even affair, with her, but she would have no part of those words. "The village is too small," she'd told him. "I cannot be seen with a *lekgoa*. When your contract is over, then who will I be? The woman whose white boyfriend left her."

Still, at the instant Kevin saw Rose, he felt a warm rush of energy along his spine and, this interested him, his sinuses. And as they nodded discreetly to each other, he had two simultaneous thoughts: "What am I, a caveman?" and "I need to get a bigger bed."

Kevin approached Kgosi Lesetedi's place just as darkness fell on the village. He paused at the entrance to the compound. "*Ko ko.*"

"*Dumela,*" came a reply from the dimly lit circle of huts. "*Tsena.*"

Kevin crouched and walked toward a circle of older men seated around a low fire. He spotted Kgosi John Lesetedi at the far end of the circle, seated on a stool slightly higher than the others. Peter Zimunya sat next to the old man, still shaken and looking for all the world as if he were sitting on a puff adder. Kevin knew the whole scene would be harder on Peter than on him, only because, and this was the irony of his life in Botswana, it was Peter's country, not his. Because he was a foreigner, he was excluded from certain culpabilities. At the same time, he knew his mistakes and inept handling of what had turned out to be an incomprehensible language made him a great source of entertainment throughout the village.

For example: Soon after his arrival, Kevin had struck up a conversation with a woman at the water pump. She'd had a baby swaddled in blankets resting on her back. In his mind, Kevin formed the sentence, "Your baby is beautiful."

"Your baby is a rabbit," he'd said.

— —

Kevin nodded at Peter, and crouched lower, eyes averted, approaching Kgosi Lesetedi while extending his right arm. "*Dumela, kgosi,*" he said.

"*Dumela ngwanaka, o tsogile jang?*" Hello, son, how did you arise? Kgosi Lesetedi asked. They shook hands.

"*Eh,*" Kevin replied. Fine.

"Sit, Mister Mahoney," Kgosi Lesetedi said. His voice was like sand and his eyes rheumy. He seemed tired. Greetings were passed between Kevin and the rest of the men. No women were visible in the circle, but Kevin knew they stood in the darkness, tending to chores, listening to every word.

"I would like to speak English," Kgosi Lesetedi said.

"We can speak Setswana," Kevin said. "I'll try."

"I don't mean to insult you," Kgosi Lesetedi said, "but we have important things to discuss. We are not talking about rabbits."

The men snickered and Kevin thought, not unkindly, at least I give these people pleasure.

"Pardon me," Kgosi Lesetedi said. "The point is, I don't want you to miss anything. Besides, I enjoy English isn't it."

Kevin looked to the other men for a reaction. Several nodded assent.

"Don't worry," Kgosi Lesetedi said. "What they don't understand, I will tell them later. English?"

"Okay," Kevin said.

"Mister Zimunya?"

"*Eh*," Peter said.

"Well, then," Kgosi Lesetedi said. He leaned forward. "What do you think of the Bruins this year?"

"Sir?"

"The ice hockey team, the Boston Bruins."

"Yes, I know them."

"You are from Boston?"

"South Boston, sir. But I don't really . . . I mean, I'm not sure."

"You are wondering how I know of this game isn't it. I know of Boston. Popcorn and hot dogs, you see. And this game fascinates me. We have all seen ice, of course, but a field of ice, a lake of ice? No, never. I can't conceive it. It is a dream of mine, to see an ice hockey field."

"Do you actually follow the team, then?" Kevin asked.

"No, in point of fact, I am a fan of the New York Rangers." He paused for effect. "You may very well ask, how is that? It would be an intelligent question."

Kevin remained silent, slightly stunned. The old men, even Peter, smiled.

"Well?" Kgosi Lesetedi said.

7

"How is that, sir?" Kevin said.

Kgosi Lesetedi leaned back into the darkness and hissed. A young girl appeared, and, as near as Kevin could understand, the kgosi told her to fetch something from inside. He leaned back. "Wait," he said, satisfied. Then, as a second thought, he leaned back into the darkness and shouted, "And bring tea!"

After a moment the girl emerged from the darkness with a shiny photo album. She dropped to one knee and handed the album to the kgosi, who took it slowly, and with some reverence. He took a pair of bent bifocals from his breast pocket and brought them to his grooved and stubbled face. Nevertheless, he squinted as he searched the album.

"Ah," he said. "There." He handed a photo to Kevin.

In the photo, a young man, as dark as a glass of merlot and made darker by the cap and gown he sported, made darker still by an overcast day, held a diploma out to the camera. He was alone in the photo.

"My son," Kgosi Lesetedi said. "The third-born. Columbia University of New York City."

The young man was long and elegant, and wore his cap at an angle. He smiled broadly. "What is his degree?" Kevin asked.

Kgosi Lesetedi frowned and leaned back into the darkness. "*A re eng?*" What did he tell us?

A woman's voice came from the darkness and filled the circle of men. "Biology," she said, in English, "pre-med."

"Precisely," Kgosi Lesetedi said. "He is still there, in New York. He is going to be a medical doctor."

Kevin nodded. "You must be proud."

"Of course. It is expected," Kgosi Lesetedi said,

softly. "And it is he who sends me news of the New York Rangers. But you know, I have always wanted to ask him something. What precisely is a hot dog?"

"Ah," Kevin said, glad he could help. "Well, it's ground meat in a tube. Sort of, I guess, like a sausage."

"Yes of course. And the meat? What type of meat is it?"

"Meat? To tell the truth," Kevin said, "I really don't know."

"Beef? Lamb? Is it in fact, perhaps, dog?"

"Dog? No, no," Kevin said. He thought about it for a moment. "God, no."

"Good. Then, why is it you call it that?"

"Well, I'm not exactly sure," Kevin said. "It's just English, I suppose. As a matter of fact, we call a lot of things 'dogs.' Feet, food, even people. It's a peculiarity."

"All languages have it, I suppose isn't it," Kgosi Lesetedi said, and he smiled. He leaned back and let out a long breath. "At any rate, you have knocked some teeth out of Mister Mdongo's head."

"Oh," Kevin said. "One tooth, actually."

— ‑

This is what Kevin knew of Kgosi John Lesetedi: He was the paramount chief of Bobokong village of northern Botswana, a man clearly venerated by his people, and, by Kevin's count, his nine living wives, fourteen living children, and uncountable grandchildren and great grandchildren. He seemed to be a man used to being loved. They said he once was tall and broad, but now he stooped slightly, and had grown a flawlessly round belly. He still showed power around the eyes and mouth.

Kgosi Lesetedi was something of an eccentric. He

9

wore several garish rings on his fingers, and had two gold teeth and a walking stick made from the mummified penis of an elephant—at least that was what he claimed. Kevin was not quite sure, he had never to his knowledge seen an elephant's penis, let alone a mummified penis, so he took the kgosi's word for it. It was long and black and had the appearance of an oversized fruit roll, and did indeed seem to be the mummified remains of something. If the kgosi was having him on, Kevin thought, so be it.

The kgosi owned a short wave radio, and listened to the news of the world daily, from Russia, the UK, France, and so on. This, even though he spoke only Setswana, English, and Afrikaans. He had learned English and Afrikaans in South Africa, during several years of education there. His English was proper, the queen's language. But he listened to the foreign language news nonetheless. It fascinated him, he said, to hear other languages.

Kgosi Lesetedi was a devout Roman Catholic, though that never stopped him from relentlessly marrying throughout his entire adult life. One of his daughters was, in fact, a Catholic nun. Kgosi Lesetedi had once told Kevin that he also listened to the news from Vatican City, for he had great admiration for the pope, who was, in his words, the most important man on earth, limited only in that he could not marry. Kgosi Lesetedi, however, suspected that the pope must have several children, because, even though it is true that we are all his children, how could he not resist having a few of his own, who looked like him? No man could.

The overriding impression Kevin had of Kgosi Lesetedi, after having lived in the village these six months, was that the chief was a powerful and slightly sad man who did not take his duties lightly, and he was a man with dignity.

—

"One tooth, actually," Kevin said.

Kgosi Lesetedi nodded his head slowly.

"I didn't intend to."

Kgosi Lesetedi turned to Peter. "Mister Zimunya?"

"Yes, I also hit him," Peter said in a tremulous voice. "I think."

"How do you think?"

"It all happened so fast."

"That is why we are here. To make it happen slowly, so we can understand. So, who would like to start?"

Kevin exchanged glances with his friend, and knew Peter would start because he was the elder of the two, by three or four years. It was custom, like children kneeling in the presence of adults. Peter cleared his throat.

"Before I begin, sir, I beg your permission. There is a problem we should soon resolve."

Kgosi Lesetedi nodded.

"It is Mister Mdongo. He is locked in the staffroom, even as we speak."

The photo album girl arrived with tea, and placed the tray behind Kgosi Lesetedi. As Peter talked, she served each man a cup of the same formula: bush tea, a dollop of sweetened condensed milk, and two spoonfuls of sugar. As always, Kevin would nurse his cup for an hour or more.

Kgosi Lesetedi frowned. "Yes, I have heard as much. It was necessary at the time isn't it. Has he been attended to?"

"He has water, and a bucket for toilet. I have instructed my girl to bring some *palache* to him later."

"What is preventing him from leaving?"

"The windows have burglar bars, and I have the key to the door in my pocket. The girl will pass the food through the windows."

"How long has he been in the room?"

Peter shrugged his shoulders, and Kevin realized he was the only one in the crowd with a watch. "About five hours," Kevin said.

"And his wounds?"

Kevin jumped in again. "I think it was only the tooth. He didn't seem to be in much pain, at least when we put him in the staffroom."

Kgosi Lesetedi sighed. "Pain has a way of coming later. You will release him after our meeting, and tell him to see me tomorrow morning."

Peter and Kevin exchanged glances. "Sir," Peter said. "He is mad."

A shimmer of amusement furrowed the kgosi's forehead, then subsided. "He has not always been mad isn't it. Now, tell your story."

Peter took a deep breath and began.

"I was in my classroom, during the afternoon study period. Mister Mahoney was in the room next to mine, with his class. Then, suddenly, from the direction of the headmaster's office, I heard a woman's scream. It was very terrible."

Kgosi Lesetedi turned to Kevin. "Mister Mahoney, you heard this as well?"

"Yes, sir." It was, as Peter had said, a chilling scream.

"So I poked my head out of the classroom," Peter

continued, "and in the next moment Miss Ndlovu burst from the headmaster's office, followed by Mister Mdongo. She was howling, and he had a hoe, a garden hoe, in his hands. He beat her on the head and body with the hoe as she ran from him—"

"Why is it that he had a garden hoe in his office?"

"Well," Peter said, "that is where we store our agricultural class supplies."

"Interesting," Kgosi Lesetedi said, stroking his chin like a detective. "Continue."

"Yes, sir," Peter said. "Anyway, he ran after her, the both of them screaming all the while."

"What did he say?" Kgosi Lesetedi asked.

"It was, ahh, something impolite."

"Which was?"

"He referred to Miss Ndlovu's mother's vagina."

A quiet murmur emitted from the men seated around the circle, signaling that some understood what had been said. A teacup clattered to its saucer.

"Then what happened?" Kgosi Lesetedi asked.

"Then, well, it all happened very fast. There was such a clamor, I am not sure. The next thing I remember was that everyone, students and all, poured out from the classrooms, and I ran with Mister Mahoney toward the headmaster and Miss Ndlovu."

Peter took a breath. "By the time we got to them, Miss Ndlovu had fallen to the ground and the hoe had broken. Mister Mdongo was beating her with the stick, and kicking her while she was on the ground. I reached him first.

"I don't recall clearly, but I think I grabbed him from behind. His eyes were black and small, and he had foam

13

on his lips, coming from the corners of his mouth. All this while the children were shouting and jeering and making a racket."

Kgosi Lesetedi shook his head from side to side and made a clucking sound. "And Mister Mahoney," he said, "you reached Mister Mdongo as well?"

Kevin cleared his throat. "Yes, Mister Zimunya held Mister Mdongo from behind. Miss Ndlovu was on the ground, bleeding, but I went to help Mister Zimunya with Mister Mdongo. He was screaming and kicking out with his feet." Mdongo was a small man, but Kevin remembered the strain in Peter's eyes and neck. "That's when Mister Mdongo bit me."

"He bit you? How extraordinary. I would like to see."

Kevin unbuttoned the top of his ugly landmark shirt and pulled it down over his shoulder. The kgosi took out his bifocals again, and stood up to examine the bite, brushing it slightly with his coarse fingers. He nodded to the men, who, in turn, stood up to examine the bite mark. Even Peter stood up to have a look.

"That is when you hit him?" Kgosi Lesetedi said, after all were settled again.

"Not exactly. I pulled his head back and pushed him away, and that is when he kicked me."

"He kicked you."

"Yes, in the . . . groin area."

The men raised some eyebrows, and Kgosi Lesetedi smiled. He turned to the men and, in the way of translation, pointed to his crotch. Several men winced.

"And that is when you hit him?" Kgosi Lesetedi asked.

"It was a reaction, more or less," Kevin said. "I didn't really think about it. I just punched out."

"Yes isn't it," Kgosi Lesetedi said, to no one in particular.

"But it had the effect of stopping Mdongo," Peter said. "He deflated in my arms, like a baby. He wasn't unconscious, he merely gave up. But he continued to shout at Miss Ndlovu as we carried him away."

"Then we carried him to the staff room, and shut him in, and locked the door," Kevin said. "We left him pacing, cursing to himself, like—"

"Like a wild animal," Kgosi Lesetedi said.

"He was mad, sir," Peter said.

"Mmm," Kgosi Lesetedi said. He reached into his back pocket and pulled out a bandana, and wiped his forehead and bifocals. He placed the rag back in his pocket, and stared at the ground, drumming his knee with his fingers. He drummed for a full minute. Kevin timed it.

"Well," Kgosi Lesetedi finally said, still staring at the ground. "It certainly has been a wretched sort of day. Mister Mahoney, I must apologize for my countryman. Now, do either of you have an idea why Mister Mdongo would attack Miss Ndlovu in such a way?"

Kevin did not. Not the slightest. So much happened—he realized this with full force now—so much happened in and around his life in Botswana about which he was utterly oblivious, that he felt like a ten-year-old in the company of adults. Which was why he knew at that instant what Peter's response had to be.

"I think I know," Peter said. He hesitated until he was sure of everyone's attention. "It was love. Mdongo had been proposing love for many months to Miss Ndlovu, and she refused him."

"Ah ha," Kgosi Lesetedi said. The other men nodded in agreement, as if this explained why a man would become perfectly demented in the middle of a working day and attempt to kill a woman with a garden hoe.

"He was taken with her, then," Kgosi Lesetedi said.

"She refused him," Peter said.

"I guess he didn't get the message," Kevin said. No one responded. "Anyway, isn't he married or something?" He winced as soon as he said it.

"He has some wives in Zimbabwe," Peter said, nonchalantly. "But they are far away."

"*Banna le basadi,*" one of the men said. Men and women. The others nodded.

Kgosi Lesetedi leaned back and sighed with some resignation, as if the incident was now in perspective. "I will hear Mister Mdongo's side of the story tomorrow isn't it," he said.

"But, I mean," Kevin said, "wives or no wives, he beat Miss Ndlovu severely. They took her to the hospital, she's there right now."

"I know this. It was my truck that took her there. One of my sons drove," Kgosi Lesetedi said. "Still, I will have to hear Mister Mdongo's side."

"And Miss Ndlovu's side," Kevin said, before he could stop himself. One of the men coughed. Peter averted his eyes.

Kgosi Lesetedi squinted, as if he'd seen Kevin for the first time. "And Miss Ndlovu's side," he said slowly. "Now, I think it is time you released Mister Mdongo. He cannot spend the night in the staffroom. Tell him to meet me first thing in the morning, and since tomorrow is Saturday, you'll have no classes to worry about isn't it."

"*Eh*," Peter said. "But, with respect, what if he is still mad?"

"He won't be. But if he is, Mister Mahoney can punch him again isn't it." Kgosi Lesetedi laughed. "The old one-two!"

Kevin forced a laugh, and the men joined in.

The meeting was over. After several minutes, Peter and Kevin excused themselves, and backed away from the circle until they reached the darkness. Peter took out his flashlight, "torch" he called it, and they walked toward the school.

"What do you make of it?" Kevin asked.

"Kgosi Lesetedi will listen to Mdongo, and Miss Ndlovu later, but I think he has his mind made up already."

"Which is?"

"Which is that Mdongo is not only a man, but he is the headmaster. Ndlovu is a teacher. There is hardly a contest. Mdongo will be punished, but lightly. He will be seen as a fool, but a fool blinded by a woman. Maybe he'll pay a small fine."

"Get out of town!" Kevin said. "You—"

"Pardon?" Peter said.

"It's an expression. What I mean is, you can't tell me that after Mdongo has beaten one of his own teachers in public, has most likely fractured her arm, he'll be allowed to return as headmaster?"

"That is exactly what I am telling you. He will probably pay a small fine, and that will be that. And what is more, Miss Ndlovu will be very happy with the judgment, I am telling you."

"How?"

"My friend, listen. Miss Ndlovu will be happy after Mdongo returns, because he will no longer bother her. She now has the power."

"Power? What power? He beat her up, not the other way around."

"Yes but he humiliated himself in public. He is a buffoon. And that is *her* power. She emerges with strength, and so do you and I, by the way. Any one of us could rub his face in cow dung now, and he would not retaliate."

"You're saying that Mdongo will never strike out at her again, not out of anger, not because of this humiliation. Not even because he is crazy. I mean, he is mad, you said it yourself."

"Yes, I said it. Who knows, maybe it was madness over a woman, not real madness. Then again, he may be a genuine lunatic. Who can tell?"

"Are you saying Kgosi Lesetedi can tell?"

"He is the kgosi. I know you don't get it," Peter said. "That is because you are from out of town. Don't worry, it is perfect."

They approached the staffroom, and noticed a small candlelight glow from within. The crowd had disappeared, and from the distance, they heard Mdongo's voice. He was singing, lightly, to himself.

"What is that?" Kevin asked.

"It is a baby's song, how do you say it?"

"A lullaby."

They reached the door. "*Ko ko*," Peter said.

The singing stopped. "*Eh*," Mdongo said.

Kevin peered inside and saw Mdongo seated, his feet up on a desk, his hands behind his neck. He was relaxed.

"Sir," Peter said through the window.

"Ah, you're here," Mdongo said, and he lowered his legs to the floor.

"Yes, sir," Peter said.

Mdongo stood up and smoothed his jacket, straightened his tie. He was a thin man, and short. He reminded Kevin of Sammy Davis Jr. He had Sammy Davis Jr.'s eyes as well, quick-moving and slightly skewed. There were small flecks of dirt and dust on his white collar, and Kevin saw a thin, dried trickle of blood at the corner of his mouth.

"May we come in?" Peter asked, in English.

"The real question, Mister Zimunya, is may I come out." Incredibly, Mdongo laughed.

"Is everything fine?" Peter asked, warily.

"Fine? Mr. Zimunya," Mdongo said from behind the door, "you sound like an airline stewardess. Yes, I am fine, if you don't count being held here against my will. I have suffered no lasting wounds. And, Mister Mahoney, the tooth seems to have come out clean, I feel no real pain."

"I'm glad to hear that," Kevin said. He debated what to say next, and went with convention. "I'm sorry."

"No, I am the one who is sorry," Mdongo said. "I believe I struck you first. And if you two are worried that I will try something, I can allay your fears. I have control. I am as calm as a sleeping baby."

Peter nodded at Kevin. Kevin shrugged.

"Mister Zimunya?" Mdongo said.

Peter fumbled with the keys for a moment, and opened the staffroom door.

Mdongo stepped out and Peter's torch displayed his smile, wide and almost silly. Mdongo clapped his hands to his chest and thumped. "Ahh!" he said. "Freedom!" He raised his arms to the night sky, as if to embrace the stars, and for one horrible moment, Kevin thought he might try to hug them both.

"Yes," Mdongo said to himself and the stars. "The jacaranda is in the air. It smells like chalk and old tea bags in there." He breathed deeply through his nose and chortled.

"I'm sorry, it was the only place we could think of." Peter's voice trailed off.

"To stash me away while I calmed down? Well, and a good thing, too. I am almost grateful you did so."

"We had no choice," Kevin said, horrified by Mdongo's composure.

"Of course not," Mdongo said, and clapped his hands together in the gesture of a person who wants to be somewhere else. He restraightened his jacket and tie, and said, "Well, it is getting late. I think a good night's sleep will do us all well."

"Kgosi Lesetedi asks that you see him first thing in the morning," Peter said.

"All the more reason for a good night's sleep," Mdongo said, not skipping a beat. He was almost jovial.

"Mister Mdongo," Kevin said. "Miss Ndlovu is in the hospital."

"Of course, of course," Mdongo said. "I've heard. They took her there in Kgosi Lesetedi's truck."

"Her arm is fractured," Kevin said.

Mdongo stopped rubbing his hands. "Then it is good she is at the hospital, I would say."

"Mister Mahoney," Peter said, "didn't you have some books you wanted to collect at my house?"

"That's all?" Kevin said, and he stepped forward. "That's all you can say?"

Peter stepped forward as well. "Mister Mahoney, I think it is time we collected those books. Good night, sir."

"Well, good night, Mister Zimunya, Mister Mahoney," Mdongo said.

"That's all you can say?" Kevin said. He felt heat across his face, and his hands were balled into fists. "That's it? Not, 'I'm sorry about the whole thing, boys'? or 'Let's hope Miss Ndlovu is okay, boys'?" He saw that Mdongo had dropped his hands to his side.

"Come, Mister Mahoney," Peter said, and he pulled Kevin's arm.

"Nothing *else* goddammit?"

Mdongo stepped back with his eyes fixed on Kevin. They were grey and empty, like bullet heads. He quickly turned into the darkness with a wave. "I can find my way. And good night again." He walked away, rubbing his hands together. Peter and Kevin stood for a moment and listened as Mdongo's shoes crunched stone and sand.

"God Jesus," Kevin said. He felt unsteady.

"You will be forgiven," Peter said. "You see? You are using your power already."

"It wasn't power,' Kevin said. He was exhausted. "So, what about you, what about your power?"

"Don't worry, I have plans," Peter said. "Now you should go home. We both should."

The two stood for a moment, and Kevin saw a shooting star arc across the southern sky and disappear into the horizon. It reminded him of Mdongo's tooth. "Which home?" Kevin said.

"You are making too much of this," Peter said.

They said their good-nights, and parted.

--

When Kevin reached his small house, he found Rose sitting in the kitchen, sipping his gin and tonic. She had lit a candle and was reading one of Kevin's books, *To Kill a Mockingbird.*

"Nice shirt," she said, and snickered.

The light glanced off Rose's high cheekbones and chin, and darkened the hollows of her eyes. Her thin fingers wrapped themselves around *Mockingbird* as if the book was a sandwich. Rose took his breath away, always, and Kevin suddenly felt vulnerable and weak. The bruise on his shoulder throbbed.

"Thanks," Kevin said. "I wore it just for you."

"Keveen," she said, "This Boo has a difficult life, would you say?"

"It gets worse," he said.

Rose cocked her head. "You look unhealthy."

"I've had a bad day."

"Come," Rose said, as she pushed away from the table. "Shall I rub your back?"

Kevin felt a need to be grounded, to regain his foundation. "Rose, what do you think about the Mdongo thing?"

Rose picked up the gin and tonic and handed it to Kevin. "I think he is a pig, and I think Miss Ndlovu was lucky that you and Zimunya were there."

"So why do I feel . . . unhealthy?"

Rose shook her head.

"Has he ever asked you out?" Kevin said.

"Who? Mdongo or Zimunya?" she said, and laughed, placing her hands over her mouth.

"Lovely. Is there a choice?"

"No. Anyway, Mdongo has proposed love to me and to every woman he has ever seen in his life. He has no boundaries, his god is between his pockets." She hesitated. "You are a hero now, did you know?"

"So I'm assuming you didn't accept," Kevin said. He sipped the warm gin and tonic.

"*Jo jo jo*," she said in a tone of disgust. "What am I, a common person?"

"It's just that you were up at the staffroom earlier."

"The whole village was there," she said. "It was a pleasure to see him locked up. If I knew he wasn't going to get out, I should have spit on him."

Kevin tried one more time. "What do you think Kgosi Lesetedi will do to Mdongo?"

"What do you mean?"

"I mean, Peter thinks Kgosi Lesetedi will let him off. That nothing much will happen, and even that Miss Ndlovu will be happy about it. Does that sound right? That the headmaster attempts to murder a teacher, and then he's let off with a slap on the wrist?"

"Slap on the wrist?" Rose said. "I doubt it. It is usually either a caning or a fine."

"It's an expression," Kevin said. "What I mean is that we'll all be back at school again, pretending nothing happened."

Rose sighed. "You are not at fault, why do you worry? He is nothing, and you saved her life."

"But, is it right?"

"Is it right? No, it is *finished*," Rose said. "You have beaten him, in front of everyone. He has been punished.

Anyway, what I think is not important. Kgosi Lesetedi will do the right thing."

"I don't doubt that," Kevin said. "I just don't get it."

"We have a proverb here," Rose said. "*Lesilo o aboela nnyo gabedi.* It means 'A fool returns to a virgin twice.'"

Kevin stared at her, dumbfounded. "What could that possibly mean?" he asked.

Rose remained silent for a moment. "Who knows? People often say proverbs at these moments, they sound interesting."

Kevin circled the kitchen and sat at the table. He gulped the gin and tonic. "Does it imply that a person can't go twice to a virgin because after the first time, she'll no longer be a virgin? Or does it mean that if you go to a virgin and she refuses you, you are a fool to go again?"

"Kevin," Rose said. "I have long ago forgotten how virgins think. It is only a proverb."

"You know," Kevin said, "it's not a bad proverb."

"Has it given you new purpose?" Rose asked. "Then I am happy I said it. Otherwise, I am sorry I said it. Come, it is late."

"Not new purpose," Kevin said. "Something." There was something, something strong about it.

"Then do not look too deeply. Leave it. Proverbs are ephemeral by nature, as are virgins. You can only be disappointed in them eventually."

"'Ephemeral'?"

Rose picked up the candle. "Don't be a snot."

"Sorry," Kevin said. "It's a fine proverb." He surprised himself by taking Rose's hand and kissing it.

Her eyes widened. "Maybe we should sleep."

"In a minute." He pulled her gently by her hand, and

encircled her waist with his arms. "You know, you really have to love this shirt."

Their faces were inches apart. "We have another proverb," Rose whispered. "Would you like to hear it?"

"Absolutely."

"*Ke tla ja ga se ke jele. Ke jele ke yo mompeng.*"

"Wait," Kevin said. "Let me try. It means 'I want you in more ways than a hyena has spots.'"

"No. It means, '"I will eat" is not "I have eaten. I have eaten" is that which is in the stomach.'"

"I was thinking that," he said.

"It is just an expression," Rose said. She held his arm, and he followed the candle's light.

END

SWIMMING

Maag, bent at the waist, dropped his shovel and placed both hands on his knees. He pushed upward, straining. It went slowly, by inches, and once upright a galaxy of darting stars crossed his pupils and he cursed himself out loud for leaving the shovel on the ground. His arms flew out instinctively for something to grab, to lean on, and the great hole he'd dug gaped before him, its dark maw ready for the moment he pitched forward.

He steadied himself, took great gulps of the hot African air, and closed his eyes. The nausea passed. He wiped the sweat from his eyebrow and, on impulse, brought his finger to his mouth to taste it. The sweat was bitter and harsh, like the skin of a mango. The chemotherapy. At that instant he sensed it, heavy, in every cell, in every pore of his skin. He imagined his cancer on a plate, the smell of it, like road kill, perverse and viscous to the touch, and his breathing shallowed, his knees buckled. His arms flailed again, and were caught by small hands from behind.

Maag shook his head to steady himself, and the boy Meshach was beside him, propping him up.

The Dane grunted. "How long you been there?"

"I am just arriving," the boy said. "Here." He bent over and picked up Maag's water bottle. His eyes were wide and somehow hopeful. "Drink."

"I'm fine," Maag said.

"Drink first."

"Goddamn cheek," Maag said, and took the plastic bottle, but there was no malice in his voice. The boy was once a student of Maag's. He came by to talk every so often. His voice was tranquil. Sometimes Maag pictured Meshach as his own son, though the boy was darker than a bottle of cabernet.

The water was warm from the late morning sun, but Maag drank it quickly. He wiped his lips and, without looking at the boy, said, "You've come again to help."

"Yes," Meshach said, and let go of Maag's arm. He gestured to the hole. "You need help."

Maag grunted again. "Yes, of course. I need help. But not with this. This is mine to do. Besides—"

"I am not too young." Meshach said, and he straightened his back. "I am thirteen. And I smoke." His brown schoolboy's shirt was threadbare, and hung from his dark shoulders like an old towel. There was dust on his tight hair and on his knobby legs from the long walk to Maag's place.

Maag shook his head. "This is, what, the third time you've asked. No. Go home now, I'll be fine."

"I am willing to work hard. Then you will teach me

28

to swim." The hopeful smile again. "I will swim in your pool."

Maag turned back to the brown hole. Moist heat drifted up from below. He thought, not for the first time, that the bottom of his hole was the only place in the Kalahari Desert where humidity existed.

He'd laid out the borders a month before, a full Olympic-length pool, fifty-five yards long and ten across. And he'd begun to dig, with a pick, a shovel, a wheelbarrow, and a water bottle by his side.

For reasons he didn't understand, he'd counted the wheelbarrows of sand and dirt he'd taken out. Three hundred and two, so far. He'd dumped each barrowful outside the chain-link fence of his compound, and by morning the sand was gone, taken by the villagers to build their chicken coops and huts.

The first layers were the most difficult, granite-hard slabs of caked sand and dust. They came out in small chunks, and with each swing of the pick the cancer sang in his belly, leaked from the growing holes in his stomach lining and intestines, and filled the rest of him with rage. And each day the swing of the pick became more fierce, and each swing was a marker against the months he had left, and with each swing he gut-stabbed the earth with his frustration and pain. Twice he'd passed out, delirious, in agony, and twice awoke at the bottom of his hole, his face and arms sunburned, bruises on his body that healed slowly, inhibited by the corrupted cells stalking his blood.

"What makes you think I'll ever finish it?" Maag said.

"Because you are the great Mista Maag," Meshach said. "You must finish it."

"You never can tell," Maag muttered, and he regretted the remark.

"You are not feeling well, Mista Maag?" Meshach said. "I think maybe you are tired from digging, and you must drink more water. See, already I am your helper. Of course you will finish. It is God's plan, He is working through you."

"God is not science, Meshach. God doesn't give a shit about me." Another wave of nausea, and the blurring. The hallucinations, or maybe they weren't hallucinations, were becoming more frequent with the chemo and doses of morphine. They were dreamlike, ethereal. When he awoke at the bottom of the hole the last time he passed out, a clump of dirt sat next to his face, and in it the perfectly formed hips and legs of the last woman who'd left him in his godforsaken desert home were spread-eagled before his nose.

"Sorry," Maag said to the boy.

"God gives a shit, you will see," Meshach said. "You are working every day until the sun goes down, sometimes even in the night. I see your lantern. It will be finished, and I will help."

"What difference does it make to you?" Maag said.

Meshach scuffed the dirt with his leathery foot, and looked down to the ground. His shoulders hunched up and down a few times. "No difference, really. I just want to help, Mista Maag."

"Don't go sentimental on me." Maag coughed. "Look, I have only one shovel."

"And I have a plan," the boy said with a brightened face. "You are too deep in the hole now to shovel out. What is it, almost three meters down?"

"In places, yes, on the deep end."

"So you dig, and fill up buckets on ropes. I will pull out the buckets and dump them into the wheelbarrow. I will carry the dirt outside of the compound. You dig, I pull. It is school break, I have time. It's a good plan."

"No. I mean, yes, it's a good plan. But you can't help."

"Why?"

"Because the village already thinks I'm a lunatic, and there's room for only one lunatic here." Obviously, an Olympic swimming pool in a small village in the middle of the great Kalahari was the pure folly of a white man. But at this point it didn't matter why he was doing it, whether the pool was his magnum opus, or simply the tangible proof of his denial. Maybe he did believe in God, just a bit. Maybe, in the deepest corner of a soul he'd denied all his life, somewhere behind his anger and grief, a miracle resided. He would have to finish it to see.

"They do not think you a lunatic. Okay, just a little. I mean, you have lived with us many years. We are used to you."

Maag contemplated the boy. He was a good son, he had a conscience, and Maag's resolve weakened. "Look, after we dig there's the smoothing out, then we have to frame the pool and pour concrete. Then we have to find some water. More water than you've ever seen in one place in your life. And get a filter. It's a lot."

The boy frowned, resolute and unblinking.

"Okay, okay, so you won't give up. I can see that. You're a regular pit bull, you are. Go home then. Come tomorrow. We'll dig."

The boy's face broadened. "Yes, Mista Maag. You'll see, we will finish quickly. With my help, we will swim in a week."

"Sure, a week. Maybe more. Now go, let me rest."

The boy was out the gate and down the path before he turned and waved. Maag lifted his arm weakly, and as the boy went out of sight he realized he couldn't move. His legs were wooden, deadened by the work and sun and everything else, and he cursed under his breath as he struggled, took a few steps, and collapsed under his orange tree.

––

Later that night, Maag lined up his chemo and morphine pills on the kitchen table. Under the murky glow of the weak light bulb, they could have been sweets arranged for party favors. One by one he took them, washed them down with warm gin. He picked up the small shaving mirror he'd taken to leaving on his kitchen table and looked at his face. A full head of graying hair and a spotty beard—he hadn't lost any hair yet—framed his tanned skin and sagging eyes, and his lips were a blunt shade of eggshell. He ticked off the rest on his fingers: Occasional though not unpleasant hallucinations, nightly post-chemo vomiting, fitful sleep, diarrhea constantly (reminder to drink more water), arms and legs as if someone had tied a sledge hammer to them, belly in a hot salsa dance. Hands blistered raw. He looked up at the wall calendar. It was labeled "Waterfalls of the World." This month was Niagara Falls, a place he'd never been, and a place that seemed, from the calendar, impossibly large. At one time people went over those falls in barrels. Of course they were idiots, risking their lives for a moment of bogus glory. Give me back my life, Maag thought bitterly, and I'd never do such a thing. He'd taken a magic marker and written, in large letters,

"SVØMME PØL" diagonally across the days. It was his reminder, as if he needed one, of his task for that month, and the next, and perhaps the next. He stood up and flipped the calendar ahead six months. Victoria Falls, in Zimbabwe, a few hundred miles north of his village and swimming pool. There were no markers on the Victoria Falls days, no reminders to do this or that, and Maag glared at the infinitely blank month. He turned to the bathroom to wait for the vomiting.

The digging went well. Meshach labored quietly beside Maag, pausing only for water and the occasional smoke. Maag smoked, too. Screw it, he wasn't afraid of getting cancer. They talked a bit, joked occasionally about the boy helping the Dane dig a swimming pool in the Kalahari. The boy's mother sent him over with lunch for two every day: fried goat meat, a pot of palache, maybe some fat cakes. Maag ate better than he had in months. In twelve days they had much of the hole dug, and Maag's legs hadn't given out once. It was as if the quotidian act of talking with someone other than himself, even a young boy, had steadied him.

During the second week they broke at noon and sat under the orange tree, dipping fat cakes in tepid, sweetened bush tea. Maag leaned against the tree and his muscles were warm, the relaxed heat of hard work. He felt that he could sleep for hours. He leaned up and, spontaneously, said, "Thank you."

"It is nothing," the boy said. "I am proud to help."

"Yes, thanks for that, too."

"Pardon?"

"Nothing," Maag said. "Listen, Meshach, I have to go to town to buy the forms and cement. It is time, I think we're nearly ready to frame the pool."

33

The boy's eye's brightened. "Yes, Mista Maag? We are ready? I told you it would happen quickly."

"You did at that, and you were right. Now, I'll travel to town tomorrow, it'll take a day to get there, and another day to buy the supplies, plus a few other things we need. I'll have to order a pool filter and some chemicals from Patel's Hardware. I'll be spending two nights in town. Why don't you take a few days off and we'll get back to work when I return."

"No. I will be the boss in your absence."

"There's nothing to do while I'm gone. Take a break, you deserve it."

"I can dig."

"Look, suit yourself, it's fine by me. Just don't knock yourself out."

"Pardon?"

"It's an American expression."

—-—

Before daybreak of the next morning, Maag loaded his Toyota pickup with three jugs of water, an extra gas tank, and his clothes, and was out of the village before dawn. The cool of the African night hung in the air, but it would be beastly hot before nine. He'd be halfway there by then, and in Kanye by early afternoon. That gave him plenty of time to do his shopping and get a cheap hotel room. The next day was reserved for a visit to his doctor, another Dane, who was not hopeful, but who dutifully wrote out the prescriptions, then filled them himself. They were the only two who knew of Maag's condition.

The veldt stretched before him, miles upon miles of sand and acacia scrub, and the road—it was a track, really, with tire spores that acted as would the rails of a train track, holding vehicles in place—was deep and rutted. At first the truck vibrated as if sitting on a magic fingers bed, then it hit soft sand and plowed through, straining and bucking for miles. The trick was to maintain momentum, to refrain from taking your foot off the accelerator. Any application of brakes was suicidal. It would bog the truck in sand, and with just a couple of vehicles headed this way each week, anyone stuck could stay that way for days. So Maag put the pedal to the floor and gripped the steering wheel for two hundred miles.

Patel was behind his counter as Maag walked in, dusty from the ride, his shirt stained by ugly rings that started under his arms and reached down to his waist. The Indian merchant smelled of curry and Brut aftershave, and he was picking his teeth with the mottled feather of a secretary bird. His eyelids were half-closed, and his thick, sensuous lips wrapped themselves around the feather.

"Maag," he said, drowsily. "Heard you're building a bloody pool."

"Is that so," Maag said. "From whom?"

"Everyone's talking about it. It's the bloody news of the century. The entire bloody desert is filled with anticipation." Then, with forced bonhomie, "Sounds like you gone bush-crazy to me, but you the man to do it."

Maag didn't like the way Patel used the word bloody, in his fake British accent. It had always been that way with the Indian.

35

"I'm the man to do it," Maag said. "And you're the man to sell me these items." He slipped a sheet of notebook paper across the counter. Then he added, "Is that all they're talking about?"

Patel raised his heavy eyelids. "Why, you got other news? Getting married finally?"

"Yes, to your sister."

The Indian snorted, ruffling the feather under his nose. "You're bloody welcome to her, get her fat arse out of my house."

"No, on second thought, life is too short. Too bloody short."

"Bloody right," Patel said as he scanned the sheet. Maag knew the man was adding figures in his head, adding an extra forty percent. "Well, we've got it all, except the pool filter and the chlorine. No one around here with a pool filter, for miles and miles. I got to order from Jo'burg."

"Fine, how long?"

"Assuming they have it, my dear friend, about three months."

Maag's nostrils sucked in a load of curried Brut. "No, it's not possible. Three weeks is more like it."

Patel gestured with the soft feather and soft hands. "Maag, Maag," he said, his voice already a slippery whine, "I'm not a bloody magician. These things take time. This is bloody Africa, you know, man?"

"It can't happen any quicker?"

"You the one building a bloody swimming pool out in the middle of Bushman land. What you expect, a miracle?"

Maag breathed deeply, suppressing an urge to spring across the counter and grapple the man's fleshy neck with both hands. "I need it in three weeks, a month at most. It's all the time I have."

"What?" More gesturing. "What you talking about? You retired, you got all the time in the world. Maybe you should have planned better."

"Then put a rush order on it."

"Or maybe you should drive to Jo'burg yourself, come back with it in three days, ey? Of course . . . " The Indian grinned, and his fat lips curled luridly, like Peter Lorre with indigestion.

"Okay, okay." Maag said. "I get it. What will it take?"

"Maag, Maag, my friend. I can say friend, yes? Sure I can move this along quickly. But a swimming pool filter is not normal out here. Big, very heavy. And a rush order, well . . . "

Maag cut him off again. "How much?"

The Indian began to crack his knuckles, first the index finger on each hand, then he moved to the middle fingers, smiling. Maag unsuppressed his urge to spring across the counter and grapple the Indian's fleshy neck with both hands. He reached over and grabbed a handful of shirt, and was nose to nose with the man's fear. "I said, how much?"

"Christ, Maag, you gone bloody mad! Let me go!"

Maag released him. "Stop cracking your goddamn knuckles."

Patel pushed himself back from the counter, straightening his shirt, his brow furrowed. "Christ, what got into you? You got the devil or something?"

"Just answer me."

The Indian continued to smooth his shirt. "Bloody hell. Three hundred should do it," he said, glancing down at his cuffs.

"Two," Maag said.

"Okay, fine, two fifty. Fuck all. Two fifty it is, now get out. Out. Come back in a week."

"Two twenty-five. And I still need the cement and frames. Nonporous cement."

"And you smell like a bloody goat," Patel said, and stepped back again. "Drive around back, my boy will load you up."

Maag walked to the door. "Oh," he said, turning, "you'll put this on my tab?"

"Sure, sure," Patel said, and waved him away.

——

When Maag returned to the village, he instantly was aware of an odd electricity in the heated air. Several villagers stopped what they were doing as he motored by on the dusty village track. They stared and waved slowly, something they rarely did, and turned quickly back to their tasks. Maag's mind raced. It had something to do with the pool.

As he pulled up to his compound he saw a small blue pickup truck parked before his house. In the driver's seat sat Kgosi Lesetedi, the chief of the village. It was the first time the chief had visited Maag's place.

Maag killed his engine and the kgosi turned and stepped from his truck. He was alone, another rarity. Kgosi Lesetedi was a big man, six feet tall with the waist of a dwarf baobab tree, and a short mat of white, curly hair covered by a knit cap. His rings, one on each finger, glittered in the early afternoon sun, and he carried, as always, an elongated, shriveled piece of flesh that served as a ceremonial cane. It was, the chief maintained, the mummified penis of an elephant.

Kgosi Lesetedi waited for Maag to greet him first, as was the custom. Maag, in a cold sweat, bowed with deference, extending his right arm while grasping its elbow with his left. The chief nodded, then inquired about the state of Maag's health and the health of his family. Maag had no family, but followed the ritual.

"Very well, thank you, all are well," Maag replied. They had switched to English, which the chief had learned in boarding schools in South Africa. The chief's eyes drooped slightly, as if he was tired, as if he'd rather have been somewhere else at the moment.

"This is a big hole," the chief said, pointing.

"Yes, it is," Maag said.

"And you are building a swimming pool," the kgosi said, in a matter-of-fact way.

"Yes."

"I should like to see it when it is completed. I have never seen such a thing. I once saw the ocean at Natal, but I have never seen a swimming pool in a man's yard. It will be impressive, I believe."

"It will be done soon," Maag said. "You are welcome to come by, to look at it any time you'd care to. Swim, even."

"Ah! Swim, never. I cannot swim and have never been in water deeper than my ankles. But, thank you, Maag. You are kind to suggest it." The chief turned to the pool and the corners of his mouth turned up.

"I know," Maag said. "I am crazy."

"Yet you are compelled to build it," the chief said. He stroked his chin with his free hand. "Why is that? What drives a man to engage in such a task? For your own pleasure? The expense is great, I'm sure. Why a pool, Maag?"

"I am not quite sure."

"Is it, perhaps, salvation?"

Maag took a deep breath and regarded the chief. "Salvation from what, Kgosi Lesetedi?"

Kgosi Lesetedi waved his hand toward the pool, the one holding the penis cane, and smiled. "Salvation from a life lived. From the devil. It hardly matters, Maag, a man's salvation is defined by the man."

"True enough," Maag said. "Then, perhaps, yes, it is. My deliverance."

Kgosi Lesetedi regarded Maag as one might a small boy standing next to spilled milk. "Good enough, then. It's a worthy task, no matter what anyone says. But, there are problems."

"I thought there might be."

"It is the boy, Meshach. His legs are broken."

"What?" Maag reeled. "How?"

"Look at your hole." The kgosi gestured again. "You see the deeper end? The dirt wall has collapsed. He was under it."

Maag stepped forward for a better look inside the hole. Indeed, the wall at the ten foot end of the pool was irregular, and great chunks of dried dirt and piled sand, taller than a man, sat on the hole's floor.

"When?" he said, and he had a hard time breathing.

"This morning. He was here at the hole digging with his brother, Abednego. He was on his knees smoothing out the corner when the wall collapsed, covered him completely. Abednego jumped in to retrieve him, and dug and pulled him out. That was when the legs broke. Or so he thinks."

"He's okay? I mean, he's talking?"

"Yes, but in great pain. We must have the legs set,

you see, but it is dangerous to drive him to Kanye. We were finally able to radio a doctor there, your friend," and here the kgosi paused, "and he is on his way. You had left already. He should be here by nightfall."

"Jesus Christ," Maag said, and his gut purled. "So the boy has been at home since this morning with two broken legs?"

"Yes, and his father is not happy. That is why I am here."

"Good God. I shouldn't have left him alone."

"Perhaps. Redemption is a difficult business. We must all be prepared for its consequences."

Maag searched the kgosi's rheumy eyes, and tried to discern his thoughts. The chief said, "Maag, why precisely did you retire from our school this year? You are not so old, not like me. I have long wanted to ask."

Maag shrugged his shoulders. "Well," he said, "it was time to build the pool."

Kgosi Lesetedi nodded, slowly. "Of course. Let us go to see Meshach."

\--

The boy sat upright on a small cot, shirtless, his swollen legs covered by a torn piece of white sheet. The open window of his hut let in air, but the boy's chest and forehead and upper lip were beaded by sweat. The hut's conical thatched roof came to a point, and a small, trapped bird fluttered above between the roughly hewn rafters. Meshach's head was tilted back as he watched the confused bird, but he smiled as Maag entered, then went back to the bird. Several people gathered around him. Maag didn't recognize them, except for the father who stood by the bed, motionless and unblinking, like a classical sculpture.

Maag and Kgosi Lesetedi and the father exchanged greetings, and the boy let the three men attend to the formalities as he followed the frustrations of the trapped bird. Finally, Maag, speaking the man's language, said, "I am sorry about your son."

The man kept his eyes on Meshach.

"I didn't think. I should have sent him home."

"Do you wish to speak?" Kgosi Lesetedi said to the man.

"I should have compensation," the father said, quietly. He refused to look at Maag. "My son cannot work, there is much to be done, and he is crippled. There will be doctor fees."

"Of course I'll pay for the doctor," Maag said. The chief raised his hand. This was his arena.

"How much?" he asked the man.

"One cow, or eight goats." The man's voice was a murmur.

"Or, money?" the chief said.

"Six hundred," the man said.

Maag glanced at Meshach, who followed the conversation intensely. The boy grimaced as he shifted on the bed.

"Six hundred is fair," Kgosi Lesetedi said. "Do you wish to speak, Mister Maag?"

"It is fair," Maag said.

"Then it is done," the chief said.

"May I speak to the boy?" Maag said. The father nodded, and several women left the bedside to make way for Maag. He sat.

"How do you feel?"

"Mista Maag," the boy whispered in English, "I am sorry. I was the boss, and I failed."

"Don't even think about it. We're fine. I am the one who is sorry. I was not there for you." He felt wet heat behind his eyes, and he snuffed. "Christ," he said.

"Don't go sentimental on me," Meshach said, but he winced. "My legs will be okay. I have eaten some bush plants from my grandmother. The pain is not so bad."

"No, the pain is enormous," Maag said. "It must be. The doctor will be here soon. I am so sorry."

"Mista Maag," the boy said. "We will have our pool soon. I will be back to help."

"Take your time, son," Maag said. "By the time you can walk about, the pool will be ready. You can come by, your whole family can come by. You'll be the first in the pool."

"May I have a cigarette?"

"Your mother wouldn't approve." He put his hand on the boy's bony arm. "Look, I must go. There's work to do."

As he stood, the trapped bird fluttered wildly, and a small feather drifted down to his shoulder. Maag reached up and took it, then slipped it into his pocket.

He left, promising the father to deliver the money in three days' time, which he did. Over the next week he dug out the fallen dirt, and smoothed the walls of the hole, then framed it. He then hired Abednego to help him pour the cement. The filter and chlorine arrived via Patel's truck, and most everything was in order. With Meshach gone, Maag ate little. He stopped taking chemo, but increased his morphine, and it hung on his arms and legs like a sodden blanket. He worked half days, collapsing into bed at two or three in the afternoon, arising at night in time to swallow some morphine. He realized, with irony, that he might be an addict.

In the fierce African sun, the cement baked dry in two days. The pool was ready to fill. Maag again hired Abednego and some village boys to carry water from the borehole, a single deep well that served the entire village. It was nearly a quarter of a mile from the borehole to Maag's pool, and the boys filled twenty-liter jugs and carried them back and forth in the wheelbarrow, all day for three days. And with each jugful of water Maag's heart beat stronger from the anticipation of it, from the weight leaving him.

On the third day he paid the boys and surveyed the clean, sparkling water of his labor, his folly; it stretched before him like a diamond runway. He dumped in a bucket of chlorine and ran an extension wire from the single outlet in his home to the filter, then went in to take a fitful nap. Late that night he gathered a chair and his morphine, a pad of paper and pen, and the feather from the trapped bird, and went to the pool. He stripped naked, stepped over the side into the cool water.

Laps. Breaststroke, head above the water. Slow laps, easy breaths, the water shimmering, crepuscular under the moon. The cleansing musk of chlorine, the filter's hum smooth and soporific. Water soughing against the sides in his wake. In the wake of his salvation.

He exited and sat drip-drying on the edge, calmed by the limpid water. When his hands were dry he walked to the chair and picked up his pad and wrote: "I, Søren Maag, being of sound mind, hereby leave my house and all its possessions including a swimming pool, and all monies garnered from bank accounts in my name, to Meshach Mpulubulusi, to be rendered to him when he reaches the age of majority. He is a fine boy, I beg that he understands. I wish a good life for him." He signed and dated it, then placed it inside an envelope along with the feather, and wrote Kgosi Lesetedi's name on the front. He pulled on a pair of shorts, and tipped the bottle of morphine tablets to his lips. It took longer than he'd thought to swallow them, but down they went, one after the other.

He gently placed the bottle and note on the ground and walked to the edge of the pool. He took a deep breath and dove, soaring into the deep end. He surfaced and turned on his back, put his hands behind his head, and floated, pleased by the speed at which the swift desert clouds covered, then unveiled, the moon.

END

JEFF CALL BETH

Kevin had rehearsed some things to say, but lost them the moment his daughter stepped out from the customs area.

"Good God," was all he said—whispered, really. Then he forgot the rest.

A stewardess walked next to his daughter with her hand on her shoulder. The girl's stiff hair lay flat and pulled back on one side, the way old photos showed Billie Holiday's sleek, burnished hair pulled tight. On the other side it was tufted and had slipped out of a ponytail, as if she'd been sleeping on it. She pushed at it lightly with thin fingers, and glanced around.

Kevin cleared his throat, and it came out like a question, an inquisitive clearing-of-the-throat. It was the best he could muster, and the girl jerked around. Immediately, Kevin saw himself in her face. He hadn't seen a photo in years, but he knew her as if he'd given birth himself, as if it was an ancient genetic connector that snaps and crackles through the air when members of the same tribe lock eyes.

Or maybe it was simply her eyes. They were dark inside and out, and tired, and glistened like pools of viscous glass. They were her mother's eyes on the day he walked out.

"Miss," he said to the stewardess. His voice wavered, slightly. "This is my daughter."

The girl's eyes widened and her nostrils flared, as if she were trying to smell something on him, or in him.

"Pardon?" the stewardess said.

"This girl is my daughter."

The stewardess turned. "Honey, is this man your father?"

The girl said, and her voice quivered as well, "I do not know him."

Kevin coughed, tried to lighten things up. "That's true," he said, to both of them. "We haven't been properly introduced." The stewardess stiffened.

"Ricky," Kevin said. "Ricky, it's me. Do you recognize me from the photos?" He'd sent photos, recent ones, of him with his wife, Gina, and their two-year-old son around the house. His life. He'd sent one Gina had taken. In it he sat with Sammy on the couch, and the boy held a small sign they'd made with crayons: "Hi Ricky. I Love You. Your Brother Sam."

The girl shrugged her shoulders.

The stewardess flicked her head, glancing from Ricky to Kevin.

"What is it?" Kevin said.

"This is unusual, that's all," she said. "My orders are to escort this girl to a Boston flight, American nine-oh-six, departing at ten thirty. Her father is supposed to meet her in Boston. I don't have any father scheduled to meet her in New York."

"I changed my mind," Kevin said. "I flew down to meet her, and I've got two seats booked on the nine-oh-six."

"That may be true," the stewardess said. "But she doesn't know you. I don't know you."

"And I'm white and she's black." Kevin said.

"Not that it matters," the stewardess said. "I mean, there's a resemblance. It's none of my business."

"Well, as you can see, she is not black, not entirely. I mean, her mother is black. Ricky, help me out here."

"I am black," Ricky said. The stewardess grunted.

"Fabulous," Kevin said.

"I have my instructions," the stewardess said.

He turned to Ricky, touched her elbow, and the girl pulled away. "Ricky," he said. "How about my voice? Don't you recognize my voice? From the phone calls?"

Ricky wore a heavy turtleneck sweater, the color of a paper shopping bag, also the color of her skin, under a light green, cotton dress he'd sent for Christmas the year before. He recognized the dress. Now it was too small, and it stretched taught across her torso, showing tufts of the sweater between the buttons.

"Your voice sounds American," Ricky said. "Inasmuch as my father is supposed to be American, you sound like him."

"*Supposed* to be American?"

"She has a point," the stewardess said.

"Please," Kevin said.

"I'm concerned for this girl's safety," the stewardess said. "That's all."

49

"Look," he said. "Would a perfect stranger walk up to a girl at an airport and claim to be her father?"

"This is New York," the stewardess said. "Does that answer your question?"

"Okay," he said. "What about my ID? You've got this father's name, don't you? Kevin Dubois?"

"You tell me. And what kind of ID?"

"A license." He reached around to his wallet.

"You don't have a passport? We prefer a passport."

"No, I don't have a passport, not with me. Listen, how about this. How else would I know this girl's just come in from Johannesburg, and that she's thirteen years old." Kevin felt the stewardess's stare as he did some mental math—he'd last seen her when she was two, eleven years ago. He turned to his daughter. "Ricky, you're thirteen, right? How else would I know all that, unless you're my daughter?"

"Everyone on this flight traveled from South Africa," the stewardess said. She leaned over and whispered. "How old are you?"

Ricky smiled. "Twelve," she said.

"Terrific," Kevin said. "Twelve it is. You're twelve, you're black, you don't recognize me, and I don't have a passport. Welcome to America."

"Thank you," Ricky said.

Then he had a thought. "Wait, how about your name? How would I know your—"

"This man is my father," Ricky said.

"How do you know?" the stewardess said.

"His voice squeaks when he is nervous," Ricky said. "This is him."

—-—

In the lounge of flight nine-oh-six, Kevin said, "You're thirteen."

"It was a test."

"You were testing me, or punishing me?"

She looked out over the crowd. "I was testing myself."

He waited for a moment.

"Of course," Ricky said, "I have passed."

—–

By the time they got to Boston and to his car, Kevin had relaxed a bit. He wanted to broach the question. He wondered if she was old enough, if she would ever be old enough. He had come to think of it in terms of a song or book title, italicized. *The Question*. It was a selfish question, and, even more, it was an intimate question. He hadn't seen this girl for eleven years; he'd never really known her. She was a small, scared stranger sitting next to him in his car.

Ricky sat silently, and the summer sun and thick sea air skimmed through the car as they approached the Massachusetts South Shore.

"Do you hate me?" Kevin said.

"What?"

"Do you hate me?"

"Should I hate you?"

"I can't answer that."

The girl was silent.

"I mean," Kevin said, "I came back to America. I left your mother. You know what I mean."

Ricky glanced out at the scrub pines clipping by, and pulled at a thread on the sweater. "These are ugly trees," she said, using the word "ugly" as one would use cherry, or oak, as if ugly was the name of the tree.

"They're common here, near the sea. You've never seen the ocean, have you?"

"I have seen it."

"Where? Cape Town? Durban?"

Ricky glanced at her watch. "*Ke nako mang?*"

"Almost noon, ten of," Kevin said.

She began to adjust her watch. "So you still speak Setswana," she said.

"I remember a bit. And your English is very good. Excellent, in fact."

"It should be so. We speak it at home. I have taken honors in it at school." She glanced out the window. "And you speak it."

They passed a distant landfill covered with swooping white gulls, so many that the dump seemed to be topped with a layer of dancing snow. Kevin waited a moment. "You haven't answered me."

"Pardon? Oh, yes, Durban."

"No, I mean about me."

Ricky stared ahead. "You are my father, and I cannot hate my father. It is written so, in the Bible."

Kevin thought about that, and let it drop.

— —

Kevin's wife, Gina, greeted them at the door. Her eyes were puffy and red, and she held Sammy on her hip. She'd cried in small, fitful jags for weeks as the visit approached, worried that Ricky, her husband's daughter from Africa, would reject her, or, at the very least, compare her to her own mother. She wanted to like the girl, not for Kevin's sake, but for her own.

Of course they'd talked about Ricky, about everything, even before they were married:

"What's she like?" Gina had said. She was asking about Ricky's mother, a woman named Siziwe.

"She's tough to describe," Kevin had said. "She's smart, well-educated, but she lied and she cheated, and she stole some things. I don't think she was all evil."

"Did you ever consider marrying her?"

"Who can tell? I couldn't have married her in South Africa, not legally, not then. But before I even thought about it, things went bad. She lied about everything. She'd go to the store for milk and be gone for three hours. She'd come back without milk. She'd say they were out of milk."

Kevin had feared, in the early days, that Gina considered him a fool, a cuckolded fool. Now he knew she wouldn't have thought that, Gina didn't think like that. Rather, she'd have felt sorry for him, as she always did. She'd simply have thought that he was a fatalist, and had too much sadness in his life.

Kevin had tried to defend it, sort of. "Things are different over there. Maybe because I'm white she felt she had to lie. Whites have always forced Africans to lie. It's implicit in the relationship. It makes whites feel safe, feel better about themselves. Our whole time together was like that, sneaking around. We lived a lie."

"And you liked living like that?"

"Well, I had a good contract. De Beers pays its engineers well, and three years wasn't a long time, not for the money. Maybe I was lonely, maybe the white girls there didn't do anything for me. I hated those accents. You don't mind that Siziwe was black, that's not it, is it?"

"No," she'd said, and Kevin always believed that to be true.

"You feel bad about it? About Ricky?"

"Only that I wish we had the first child together. Our first, and yours."

"We didn't plan it," Kevin had said, "or, I didn't plan it. Siziwe was on the pill. I found one on my bathroom floor one day. I asked her about it. She said she didn't know, maybe it belonged to someone else, the maid or someone. Two months later she was pregnant."

"Kevin," Gina had said, "let me paint this picture for you. Your girlfriend is showing up at all hours, and she's a liar to boot. She's dumping her contraceptives down the toilet and gets pregnant. Then she tells you it's your child."

"It sounds bad, I know," he'd said. "I had tests done. Siziwe didn't like it, but I did it anyway. There's no question. And someday, when you see Ricky, there'll be no question."

"She flushed the pills to get pregnant. She was evil," Gina had said. "I'm sorry to have to sound like a jealous bitch."

"Well, she lied like hell," Kevin had said.

—⁃—

Gina needn't have worried about Ricky. The girl greeted her with a full measure of respect, curtseying at the door and extending her right hand while touching her elbow with her left.

"You have a big house," she said, and giggled.

54

"It's not big," Gina said. "It's just that people are so small. We are so very happy to have you."

"Thank you," Ricky said. "I, too, am happy to be here." Gina smiled at Kevin.

"This is Sammy?" Ricky said, holding out her hands for the boy. She took him and smiled and looked into his brown eyes. The boy touched her hair. She greeted him formally in her language. "*Dumela rra*, hello Sammy. He is a pretty boy. He looks just like you," she said to Gina.

"He has your father's eyes," Gina said. "Like you."

"No," Ricky said. "He looks like you."

Gina glanced at Kevin. "I'll get the luggage," he said.

Later, Kevin picked up lobsters. At dinnertime they all gathered in the kitchen, tossing salads, buttering garlic bread, and shooing Sammy out from underfoot. South African township music played in the background on an old cassette Kevin had brought home, Letta Mbulu singing "I Need You." Ricky sang along, and chatted, mostly, to Gina. It was a family scene with a twist, and Kevin caught himself glancing at his daughter, hoping she'd say something to him, even look his way.

Kevin put on a pot of water, and when he brought a lobster out of the bag, Ricky sucked her teeth and looked his way.

"What is this?"

"A lobster," Kevin said. "From the sea."

"It looks like a big insect," Ricky said.

"It is, sort of," Kevin said. "A sea insect."

"You eat it?"

"Yes, and you'll eat it as well."

"No."

"Taste it?"

"Uh-uh." By that she meant "no."

"I got it especially for you. It's sort of a traditional food around here. At least in the summertime."

"It still looks like an insect."

"People eat insects at your home, don't they? Termites?"

Ricky was horrified. "Common people eat them. I do not." Kevin glanced at Gina. He needed some help.

"Well," Gina said. "We'll cook it, and if you want to taste it, you can, no pressure. We'll make something you like tomorrow night." And Kevin shoved a squirming lobster into the pot.

Ricky stood rigid. "You don't kill it first?"

Kevin cleared his throat. "It dies in the pot."

Ricky leaned over and looked at the lobster, now turning pink. "No screams? A big thing like that?" she said.

"I'll make you a hamburger," Kevin said.

--

Later, after Ricky changed into her nightclothes, Kevin knocked on the door.

"*Tsena*," Ricky said.

Kevin opened the door and said, "Everything okay?"

"Yes." She was sitting on the bed, cross-legged, brushing her hair. She had just spritzed herself with perfume. It was the same perfume her mother used. She didn't look up.

"Comfortable?"

"Yes."

"Do you want to talk? Read a story or something?"

"Uh-uh." No.

"Does your mother read you stories?"

"Which stories?"

"Bedtime stories. Kids' stories. That sort of thing."

"She tells them, she doesn't read them."

"Okay, do you want hear a story?"

"She stopped that years ago. I am old."

"You're not that old."

"I am too old for stories. I know them all. I have heard them all."

"No one is too old for stories," Kevin said. He sat down on the edge of the bed. "Anyway, it's okay. I guess I'm new at this. Does your mother kiss you goodnight, tuck you in?"

Ricky glanced at him quickly, then looked away. She patted the hair on top of her head. "Here," she said.

"She kisses you there?"

"Sometimes. Just there." She kept her head down, as if she were walking in the rain.

"Okay," Kevin said. "May I?"

"It is up to you."

Kevin stood up and kissed the top of her head. Her hair was warm, and smelled like dry earth.

--

Early the next morning Kevin set up a call to Siziwe, to let her know Ricky had arrived safely. He gathered his family around the table, at breakfast. It was afternoon in Johannesburg.

"*Dumela, rra,*" Siziwe said. The line was hollow, tinny.

"*Dumela,*" Kevin said. "How are you?"

"Fine," she said. "Very well. It's months since we talked. You sound healthy. Strong."

"Yes, I'm fine, thanks."

57

"What do you look like these days?"

"Pardon?"

"What do you look like? You were once slim, have you grown fat?"

"Comfortable, I guess. I'm not sure."

"You can't talk? Won't talk?"

"Does it matter?"

"Your wife is there."

"Yes," Kevin said. "She is."

"So," Siziwe said after a pause, "Ricky is finally in big, busy America, with her big, busy daddy. She must be thrilled."

"I wouldn't say that, precisely."

"Really? Is she resisting your charms? I find that hard to believe. By the way, I still hate you, do you still hate me?"

"I never did."

"Of course you did. It was fated to be that way."

"No, it wasn't." From the corner of his eye, he caught a puzzled look from Gina. And from Ricky.

"Then it must be my fault," Siziwe said. "I invented hate. Don't worry, I have resigned myself, long ago."

"Please," Kevin said. He glanced at Ricky.

"And do you know what?" Siziwe said.

"I'm sure I don't."

"You hate Ricky, too."

He turned his back to his family, and hissed into the phone. "What?"

"You hate her because she was born, because she came between us."

Kevin lost his breath for a moment. A dull, vulgar pain nipped at the base of his throat.

"I am correct, am I not?" Siziwe said. "You hate

her for what she is. Our little reminder. She is our doppelgänger."

Ricky tapped Kevin on the back, and when he turned her hand was out for the phone. She rolled her eyes in a sympathetic gesture.

"Look," he said, and his voice sounded feeble, "Ricky is standing by."

"Of course, as always. You infuriate me. Let me talk to my daughter."

Kevin handed the phone to Ricky, and the two talked for fifteen minutes in Setswana. Ricky glanced at Kevin as she spoke—she raised her voice once—and again as she hung up.

"Everything okay?" Kevin said.

"The same," Ricky said.

Soon, they developed a routine. Kevin went to work while Ricky was still in bed. He'd call home about ten in the morning, when he was sure she was up. They'd have abbreviated conversations, as in, "Did you sleep well? Yes. Going shopping with Gina today? Yes," and so on.

Later Kevin would come home, and after dinner take Ricky and Sammy to the town playground for the last few hours of summer light. Ricky smiled more, laughed harder, at the playground. She would play with Sammy, ride down the slide with him, and watch after him while Kevin walked down to the corner 7-Eleven to bring back a couple of Slurpees.

Sometimes, she would get into a swing. "Push me," she'd say.

Kevin would push. He'd stand behind and press gently at her back, more a prod, an urge, than a push. Ricky's muscles were taut, and her shirt was always damp from the running. Then he'd push harder, and

Ricky would shriek like the child she was, her shiny legs pointed to the orange sky. "Higher!" she'd shout, and Kevin would give her a hard shove, so hard they would both exhale loudly as she left his hands. "Higher!" she'd shout again, and he'd push like a madman, running with the swing, his hands on her back. Then he'd push again and run, ducking and coming out beneath her legs as she swooshed back, giggling and faking an attempt to kick him.

After she got off the swing, she would pull away if he tried to hold her hand, or touch her in any way.

—-

"She can't stand me," Kevin said one day, after the kids were in bed.

"I don't know," Gina said. "You know how they say that muggers spot victims by the way they hunch over and cross the street and walk scared? Almost as if the victims choose to be mugged."

"That's a stretch," Kevin said.

"Well, maybe it's true. Anyway, you're getting from her what you give, which is guilt and anxiety."

"We're Catholic, what else is there? How are you two getting along?"

"Fine. She's almost a teenager, she can be a snot sometimes. I talked to her about how she treats you."

"Really? What did you say?"

"I told her that you were trying the best you know. I told her that she might try to cut you some slack, that it might be difficult at times to catch up with each other."

"What did she say?"

"She just nodded."

"I'm not surprised."

"Then she told me that her hair used to be short, like in her passport photo."

"Yes, I know," Kevin said.

"She said that we kept sending her things for her hair, like ribbons and clips and shampoo and whatever. So she figured you had this thing about hair, about her hair."

"They were just small things to send."

"Well, it seemed to her that you had something about hair. So she grew her hair out. She thought you'd like it. She did it for you."

Kevin swallowed, and it hurt. "You're kidding."

"No," Gina said. "I'm not. Anyway, she likes me, and that's because I like her."

"I like her, too," Kevin said.

"Do you? Or, do you want to love her so desperately you can't tell?"

"What else can I do?"

"Admit it and face the truth. Maybe you like her and maybe you don't. Maybe the same is true for her. Clean your soul. Start fresh, whatever you want to call it. Act like a guy. Tell me, for instance, that you still feel something for Siziwe."

"What?"

"I think you heard me. You owe me this."

"Well," Kevin said, sorting it out as he spoke. "Maybe a residual fondness. We had a kid together."

"I'm not blaming you. I'm not saying if she walked into this room right now that you'd swoon dead away. But you *feel* something for her, am I right?"

"Feel, like what? Like I want to screw her? Take care of her? Like what?"

"Like the heat," Gina said, and she leaned close and

smiled. "The heat at the back of your eyes when you think about it."

––

They bought a bike for Ricky, and they took rides through the trails and bike paths of their small town. They went on picnics, and took her to the beach, where invariably she was one of two or three blacks there. She would glance quickly at them and they at her. Whites gave them liberal nonchalance and a smile, as if they were looking at a Norman Rockwell scene for the multicultural day, a social worker with an inner-city kid out to the beach for the day.

Except for the two girls. It happened about midvisit. The two girls—they might have been eighteen or so, and they were both overweight, enough so that they attracted stares—both wore black oversize T-shirts over their suits. They ambled up the beach, laughing much too loudly for big people, and gesturing with their cigarettes. When they came upon Sammy and Ricky building a sand house at the water's edge, they slowed and whispered to each other. They walked by and hissed something, and Ricky's head snapped up as they passed. Kevin got up from his lounge chair.

"What did she say?" he said.

"She told her friend to watch out, someone left a shit in the sand," Ricky said, and her eyes narrowed.

"You're kidding," Kevin said. "You know the word?"

"I know it."

"They said it just like that?"

"Yes, like that." The two girls were about fifty yards down the beach. Sammy pushed some sand into the hole.

"Let me take care of it."

62

"No," Ricky said. "No, it is okay." But she had begun to cry, and Kevin reached for her shoulder. "No," she said, and shrugged hard.

Then Gina was at his side. "Take Sammy," she said gently. "Let me talk to her."

"No," Kevin said. "I'll be right back."

"Don't do it," Gina said. "You'll only embarrass her."

But Kevin was already on his way, tailing the two girls. He moved quickly, kept his head low, and listened to his heart thump as his rage grew. The two girls glanced back once or twice, but didn't seem to recognize him as being connected to Ricky. He started to rehearse some things to say, but lost them the moment he caught up.

"Hey," he said.

They turned and stopped. "Hey, what?" one of them said. She sneered, and that, incomprehensibly, made Kevin relax.

"You know," Kevin said, "I wouldn't have believed it if I hadn't seen it with my own eyes, but you two are enormous."

"What?" the other one said.

"Enormous, is what I said. Obese. Corpulent. Mountainous."

"Fuck off," the sneering girl said. A couple of heads turned on the beach.

"Oleaginous," Kevin said. "Goddamn fat. Together you could be a small county."

Both girls gaped. Kevin cleared his throat. "Thank you for helping," he said. "You'll never know."

He left the girls blinking, and found Ricky and Sammy sitting in the sand. Gina stood over them, and her brow was wrinkled. Kevin winked.

"Ricky," he said. His daughter looked up. "Did I ever tell you how much I like your hair?"

"No," Ricky said. "You never did."

——

Despite the anxiety, or perhaps because of it, the visit moved quickly. Before he was prepared for her departure—whatever that meant, and he wasn't sure, just as he had never been sure what her arrival meant—it was time to take Ricky for the last round of clothes shopping, the last round of chocolates, the last visit to the hair salon, the last night. They gave her the choice of restaurant and activities. She chose McDonalds and bowling, which she'd heard of but never done. They had a hoot. They wantonly threw balls down the gutter, they screamed at strikes, Sammy ran down the alley after the balls. Kevin felt something good was happening, something positive, as if a cool and wet wind had started to blow through a hot, oppressive day.

Ricky asked Kevin for a few dollars to get some sodas. He gave her the money, and when she returned, she smacked the back of his head hard—it was a "*thwack*!", he saw it in his mind's eye, like a background noise splattered across the evil character in a Batman comics strip—with her open palm. It stung and he spun around, but she was laughing. Gina opened her mouth, but checked herself, confused by the merriment.

"What the hell was that for?" Kevin said.

"Too hard?" Ricky said.

"Yes," Kevin said, rubbing his head, "too hard."

"I'm sorry," she said, and she giggled. Sammy giggled.

Kevin held up his hand to Gina, to stop her. "It's okay," he said to anyone, and everyone.

The next morning, the day of Ricky's departure, the air was crisp, a late-August reminder of fall. They ate silently, then Kevin loaded the car. The goodbyes were brief and Sammy suffered the worst. He sensed the discomfort, and when his mother began to weep, he wept, as did Ricky. In a moment, Sammy began to bawl and hiccup, and Gina sobbed while Ricky pawed gently at her face. Gina pulled Ricky in, and they hugged, with Sammy sandwiched in the middle and Kevin hovering on the outside. Then, except for the sobs, they all fell silent.

Finally, Gina said, "There's always a place for you here."

"Yes," Ricky said.

"I'm so happy to finally have met you," Gina said. "You'll come next year? Maybe in a couple of years?"

"Yes," Ricky said, and she pushed Sammy's tears down his face.

"Let's go," Kevin said.

They got into the car and waved, and Ricky blew kisses and stared at Gina and Sammy until they were out of sight.

Kevin made a snap decision to stay off the highway and on the back roads as they headed north to Logan Airport. He needed to relax, and he wanted to talk. He tried to remember what it was that he'd been wanting to say to Ricky during the past month, during her entire life. He tried to form some words, but felt left out, vacant, on the fringe, as if he wasn't there. Ricky hummed a muted tune and watched the small farms and neat New England houses click past her window.

They turned a corner on a small hillock and passed a makeshift sign, bare plywood with painted black, ragged letters, like the kind that would usually say, "Tag Sale Saturday 9–3. No early-birds." But this one said, "Jeff Call Beth."

Ricky turned her head as it blurred by.

"What does that mean?" she said.

"That sign? It looks like someone wants Jeff to call Beth."

"Who are those people?"

"I'm sure they know who they are. It's a message between them."

"But, who wants Jeff to call Beth?"

"I don't know. Maybe a friend. Maybe it's Beth herself."

"I don't understand," Ricky said. "Why would someone make a sign like that?"

Kevin considered some possibilities. It was an odd sign, now that Ricky mentioned it. "Sometimes people do things like that," he said, "to make a point."

"But," Ricky said, "out on the street like that, for all the world to see? This is no way to send a message. Why not call him on the telephone?"

"I don't know."

"And why should Jeff call Beth? Why not Beth call Jeff?"

"Well, maybe Jeff has no phone."

"Then how is he to call Beth?"

"I don't know. A pay phone?"

Ricky fell silent, then leaned forward in her seat. "It makes no sense," she said, sounding anxious. "Maybe Jeff doesn't want to call Beth. Has anyone even considered this? Maybe he has no reason to call Beth. Maybe he doesn't even want to talk to her."

"Well," Kevin said, and he lowered his voice, "maybe she wants to get in touch with him, but is afraid to call him directly. Maybe she's shy."

"She is a fool," Ricky said. "*Mosetsana o motlhanka.*" This meant, "The girl is a slave."

"And anyway," Ricky said, "how is she to know Jeff will see the sign?" She was animated.

"Well, she must know something about him. Maybe he drives by here every day."

"So she leaves the sign up for—how long? Months? Years? Until he calls? I cannot imagine such a thing. She is desperate."

"Is that bad?" Kevin said.

"Yes, of course! Can't you see?" She'd begun to raise her voice.

"I don't know," Kevin said. "Sometimes desperation helps people to do things they wouldn't normally do. Important things."

"But where is her pride!" She was shouting now. "This is an embarrassing sign. She makes herself weak, like a child, as if she is telling the world she is pathetic!"

"Perhaps Beth didn't make the sign. What if, say, a friend of the two of them wanted them to get together, or get back together, and thought this was the best way to do it?"

"Then this friend is no friend!" she shouted. She clapped her hands together in a manner of dismissal, and her voice reverberated in the car.

Kevin stayed silent for a moment. Ricky breathed heavily through her nose, and her chest rose and fell.

67

"She's reaching out the only way she knows," Kevin said. "Don't be so hard on her."

Ricky balled her fists and smashed them into the dashboard. "*What do you know about her!*" she snarled. Her face screwed tight. "*What could you know about Beth*! You don't know. You know nothing about her life! You don't! *You know nothing about her!*" She turned to him and her eyes blazed for a second before she lurched forward and threw her face into her hands, sobbing.

After a moment, Kevin reached out and gently touched Ricky's heaving back. "Ricky," he said.

She mumbled something, but her hand muffled her quivering voice.

"Ricky," he said.

And then he found his voice.

END

COLD ON ICE

I parked my car on a small dirt path that turned off from the main road, and before I got out I rolled down the window and listened. The only sound was the cracking of the vinyl as I shifted in my seat. It was five-thirty in the morning, a black winter morning, and the time seemed right so I picked up the skates and coffee and tightened my wool scarf, and walked down to the pond.

I stood at the crusted shore, breathed through my nose, sipped some coffee. Sometimes, it seems to me, it's not what you hear, it's what you don't hear. Silence is God's gift to the weary. Linda, back at home, was hearing nothing, too. She was asleep, and I'd kissed her lightly before I left the house. She'd wake up with the taste of coffee, cream, two sugars on her lips.

I decided to wait till the sun came up a bit, give me a little light, so I sat down on a rock. There was time, and I had nothing if not time for this. Steam from the coffee whorled around my nose and eyes, and I kept the skates in my lap. They were Freddy's skates, but of course he'd never wear them. I'd never shown him the skates, that would've served no purpose, and would've been thoughtless and impulsive. What could I have said? "Here, Freddy, I bought you these skates when you were born because I myself loved skating when I was a kid, but you'll never know that pleasure so just the same I thought I'd show them to you"? No, of course not, though God knows I'd wanted to show him the skates, show him something, every day since he was born.

We'd worked it into our lives. We had routines, we had things we did. We had things that made Freddy, made the three of us, laugh. His doctor once told me it's like a child born blind: they adjust and never miss seeing because they never did, and Freddy never misses walking because he never did. Of course I don't buy that completely. Freddy sees the other kids walking and running. Skating. He doesn't complain much, but no doctor can tell me he doesn't long for it, doesn't want working legs in his life, doesn't want to get out of the wheelchair. I know he does; I see it every time I look into the mirror.

Still, Freddy has important business these days.

Freddy plays the violin like a man possessed. Or, a boy possessed. Linda bought him a violin six years ago, when he was four, *on a whim*, and he took to it like cold on ice. At first he just fooled around with it, made noise, figured out a few notes, then chords. Then he started to play along with the classical station on the radio. Soon he wanted lessons, he wanted more, pleaded for more. He spent, and still spends, half a day on the violin, listening to classical CDs, playing along with string parts, practicing his lessons. His teacher costs enough, but we've been sponsored by a grant from the Hartford Symphony, with whom he practices and plays once in a while. He plays on radio programs, once went to New York to play on Regis and Kathie Lee. His hero is Papa John Creach, who is dead, but whose old albums I have from his days with Hot Tuna. Freddy's face lights up over that violin, and Linda lights up, too.

The skates are adult-size hockey skates, Bauer Airs, the best on the market. I bought them before he was born, thinking Freddy would be a real hotshot on his high school hockey team. That was my game, hockey, in Albany when I was a boy. The skates fit me, I've tried them on.

So I sat at the side of the frozen pond, listening to nothing, waiting for the sun, waiting for my time. I finished the coffee and laced on the skates. They were tight, so I took them off and pulled up my socks, and tried them again. They hurt a bit, so I flexed my ankles and stretched the leather, and waited for the sun.

My aim was to skate around the pond, to circumnavigate it, let the wind score my face as I pushed myself from one end to the other and back again, maybe around and back another time. The only sound would be the chunk of the skates on ice and my breathing—the silence would be key to all this—and I would force myself to come to an understanding about Freddy, about how he would be in that wheelchair for his life, no question about it, it's a fact. I had always, since the moment we heard the news, hoped for a miracle. But it wasn't going to happen, I knew that now.

So I planned to skate to reality. I would skate and roll it all together and let it go, feel sorry for us for the last time. I'd skate and shed the ache and grief and anger

71

like a bad skin. And when the spring thaw came it would melt with the ice and the grieving would sink to the bottom of the pond, and that would be that, and I would somehow be freer than I was before, even freer than before Freddy came into our lives.

I was going to take off the skates and leave them at the side of the pond. Maybe a kid would find them, try them on, take them, never have to know Freddy's saga. It seemed the best way to handle the skates part of it.

I heard a car out on the main road. It broke the silence, and I hoped it would pass, but it turned down the side road where I'd turned, and its headlights briefly swept across the black pond. The engine cut out, and in a moment I heard a car door slam. A man whistled softly to himself.

In a minute or two I saw him, about fifty yards to my right, at the side of the pond. The morning light was breaking, and I made out the shadow of a fishing pole and a wooden box he carried, about the size of an old-fashioned milk box. The guy was about to do some ice fishing. He hesitated, then stepped onto the ice. He was of average size, about six feet, with a heavy parka and calf-length rubber boots. The coat hood was pulled up over his head. He walked like people in flat soles walk on ice, a sort of small-step shuffle as he made his way toward the center of the pond. He looked neither left nor right, and I was sure he hadn't seen me, although he must have seen my car and knew I was around somewhere. I cursed to myself, thought I would miss my chance to skate the pond alone and deliver Freddy's skates.

I decided to wait it out. Maybe the guy wouldn't have any luck, or maybe he'd get cold waiting for the trout, leave in a few minutes. Although, no fisherman worth anything would wait less than an hour. But I had time. I watched the guy shuffle for a while, and finally he stopped near the center of the pond, assessed a spot on the ice, and put down the box and his rig. He leaned over and flipped open the lid, pulled out a hand drill. It was the big bent kind, shaped like one of those fake comic arrows that you put on your head to make it look like it went right through one temple and out the other. He pushed the box closer, sat on it, and lowered the drill to the ice. As he started to turn the handle and grind away at the ice, I tried to figure this out. The drill bit was, what, no more than an inch, and I couldn't see what kind of a fishing hole it would make. I saw no pick, no shovel, just the fishing rig.

After about five minutes the guy stood up. The sun was high enough to make out the color of his coat—it was dark crimson—and he leaned back, as if to crack his back, as if the drilling was an effort. He kicked the box hard, pushing it back twenty feet, and picked up his rod and shoved it along the ice's surface in the direction of the box. It skittered and came to rest by the box. Then he took off his glove and reached into his coat pocket and took out a small object, bent over, and placed it where he'd been drilling. Without standing up, he reached into the pocket again and took out a lighter, which he fiddled with for a moment before it lit and he extended his hand to the small hole in the ice. He stood up and shuffled quickly backward, away from the hole. A small fuse sputtered on the ice's surface, and I braced myself.

A small geyser flecked with ice chunks erupted from the hole a split second before the sound hit me. It was more than I'd expected, a sharp crack—an M-80 I figured—and the sound echoed off the trees along the pond's edge, reverberating through the mottled gray of the morning. Birds screamed and took off from the treetops. It took me by surprise, and my feet shot out. The skates' blades crunched the frozen mud underneath the rock.

After the sound died off, the guy slid one foot forward toward the hole, leaned on it, testing the ice. When he was satisfied, he slid the other foot forward. He was a cautious man. He got to the hole, now a decent fishing size I reckoned, and peered into it. He bounced a bit at the edge of the hole, testing again. Then he turned back, fetched his rod and box, and shuffled back to the hole. He sat on the box and unhooked his line, dropped it down into the hole. It was already baited up and ready to go.

Settling in, I thought. It's cold out here, and this could be a long wait, maybe best to come back tomorrow morning. Freddy and I have waited for ten years, we can wait another day. I made the decision right then to leave, and as I leaned over to untie the skates, I saw him from the corner of my eye, a blurred crimson shape hunched over, steam coming from beneath the hood.

The ice cracked. At first it was a small, rumbling crunch like a car on gravel. I looked up, and the guy was up, too, just coming off the box, when the ice cracked again. This time it snapped with a hollow sound, like a belt strap against an empty oil drum. The man went down into the water. He went down slowly at first, flailing his arms as he tried to lean back and fall on solid ice. But he was in too deep, too close to the edge of the hole. The ice cracked behind him. He sank to his waist and shouted, "Oh Christ!" But he held onto the fishing rod.

The water gurgled softly as he sank, and he shouted

again. His voice was pitched high, and desperate. "God-dammit! Help!"

"Hold on," I yelled. The skates were still on, still laced. "Hold on." I wobbled onto the ice, then pushed off with my right foot, the way I always did, thirty years before, when I was a boy on Albany ice. I shooshed off, glided, pushed with my left, then right, then left again, picking up speed. I was, in the silent part of the mind that never speaks, aware that I did pretty well for a man who hadn't been on ice for years. The guy was maybe half a football field's distance out, and I skated like a madman, banging and grabbing the ice with my toes, slamming my skates to get to him.

As I skated closer, I heard his muffled sobs, desperate sobs. "Oh, Christ, oh no," he said. He'd seen me skating toward him, and reached with the hand that wasn't holding the rod. He was in past his waist, sinking, the weight of his clothes pulling him down. "Help me," he said as I got to him. I stopped about ten feet short. His eyes were wild with fear.

"Don't worry," I called out. "We'll think of something." But I couldn't think of anything. I knew that if I got too close, the damaged ice would give in and I'd go into the water. Both of us would sink to the bottom of the pond and we'd be headlines the next morning, "Two Men Sink to Icy Deaths." I had to stay a safe distance. My lungs felt raw and my heart pounded, from the skating and from the danger in front of me.

"Pull me out!" the man said. He gasped for air; he was out of breath, too.

"What kind of rod is that?" I said. He was still holding on to it, although I'm not sure he was aware of that.

"What?" he said. "Fishing, fishing rod."

75

"Sections or solid?" I said. In a suddenly vivid corner of my mind a plan started to formulate. I remembered this story I'd read about polar bears, about how they never break through thin ice, even though they weigh close to a ton. They flatten themselves out completely, distribute their weight, and inch slowly across by shoving lightly with their legs and arms. I remembered that when I read that story the first thing I thought was that those bears were patient. They were diligent.

His eyes scrunched for a moment; whether he was remembering or incredulous at the line of questions, I didn't know. "Solid," he said. "Help me!"

"Good. Kick off your boots," I said, "and keep holding on to that rod. Can you kick off your boots?"

"Okay," he said, and he was out of breath some more. He struggled, his legs underwater, working at the boots. It was about half a minute, and he closed his eyes and cried as he kicked away. He held onto the ice's edge with his free hand and held onto the rod with the other. His action churned the water like it was at a slow boil. "Off," he said, finally.

"Okay," I said, "now let me grab the end of the rod. Don't let go of your end."

So I got down on my belly, every inch of me flat on the ice like a polar bear, and slowly made my way toward him, testing it. My nose sent large streams of steam onto its surface. I got to the rod and grabbed the end. It wasn't much of a hold, but was the best I could do. As long as he didn't let go of his end, he wouldn't sink. I stayed on my belly, parceling out my weight across the ice. "Can you take off your coat? Use one hand at a time."

"My hands," the man said. It was plaintive but a

statement, as if he needed to remind himself that he had hands.

"Don't give up," I said. "We're almost there. Work on that coat, keep your gloves on." He reached with his free hand and unzipped the heavy parka, and he winced as his arm went below the water. "Slip your arm out of the coat and then grab the rod with that hand. Then take the coat off the other arm." He slipped out his free arm, and I was amazed, and happy, at how easily the coat dropped away from his shoulder. He switched hands on the rod, whimpering, and then his back was to me.

"Too cold," he said. "My feet."

"Drop the coat," I shouted. "Or you'll die. Do it. Now." The man was fading fast, from the cold and from the desperation. He whimpered again. "Oh, God." But he shook the free arm, shook it hard in one last effort, and the coat slid off his other shoulder and into the water between him and the jagged ice at the hole's edge.

"Good," I said, "now grab that rod with both hands. Grab it and grab it good. Don't pull, just hold on." He swung back and grabbed the rod. "Please," he said, and his voice was low, almost a whisper.

I flipped over on my back, still flat to keep my weight distributed, still holding the rod with both hands. I extended my feet, raised my legs high, and let them come down, hard. The heel ends of the blades dug into the ice. Then I started to bend my knees up, slowly, using the dug-in skates as an anchor. I pulled forward with my legs and arms. "Don't let go of that rod," I said to the sky. "And don't pull back."

The man came out a bit, and he was heavy, heavier than I expected, but it would've been worse with the boots and parka. I felt the sweat beneath my gloves, worried they'd pop off. I pulled forward, breathing hard. "Don't move," I said. I raised my legs again, and let them come down, digging in. We'd gained about six inches. "Don't move," I said again.

I repeated the process, shouting at the guy to hold on. He did, and didn't pull back, almost as if he was frozen to that fishing pole. He came up slowly, dead weight at the end of a light stick, another six inches. I kicked my legs forward and did it again, digging those skates in and pulling with my legs and arms. My legs throbbed at the thighs, started to cramp. I turned my head back over my shoulder, and I saw that the guy was almost half on the ice, at least his chest was up out of the water. "Please," he whispered.

"One more time," I said. "At least." I slid forward on my back and dug in my heels again. "Don't let go," I said. I pulled, with my arms and my legs, and I heard water splash. "Goddammit," I said, "move." I gave it an almighty effort, pulling with my entire body, and I heard myself grunt. I turned, and the guy was on his belly on the ice, his legs were still in the water from the knees down. "Good," I said.

I turned and sat up, still holding my end of the pole, and faced him. Then I dug in the blades at the heels, like I was on a rowing machine. "Do not pull," I said. "Here we go, hang on." I pulled, slowly, and pushed back with my legs at the same time, listened for cracking ice. The man stayed on his belly, and in a minute he was out, his red, woolen socks dripping water into the hole he'd blown into the ice. "Don't move," I said. I slid back a foot, pulled again with my arms and legs. He slid away from the hole, his wet clothes leaving trails on the ice. "I'm going to do that again," I said. "Hold on." I pulled again, he slid again, and I stayed dug in, kept pulling the rod, until the guy was at my feet, prostrate. "Oh, God," he said.

"Don't stand," I said, but he couldn't have moved if I'd asked him to. I couldn't move. My legs were cramped, and my hands and arms were knotted by locked muscles. "Just wait a minute."

We both did that, wheezing, the guy starting to cry. "I don't trust this ice," I said. I dropped the rod and grabbed the collar of his flannel shirt, dragged him farther away. "Let go of the rod," I said. "We're okay now." He let go, and the rod stayed on the ice, and he sobbed.

The guy had been in the water maybe five minutes, maybe less, but he was in shock and in pain. We had to move, and I grabbed his collar again. "Can you walk?"

"No," he sobbed, "no legs." So I dragged him, in fits and starts, slipping on the skates, falling, him on his belly on the ice, me with my hand on his collar, to the shore. It took an ungodly time, and by the time we reached the shore my legs were numb. We stopped by the rock and my coffee cup.

"You've got to try and walk," I said. Steam drifted up from beneath my sweater, from around my neck and my face. "You've got to try and walk, we're off the ice here. I'll help." The cars were another fifty feet or so, up a small dirt path from the pond.

"Okay," he said. "Okay." He rolled over on his back, his face crimson, like his discarded parka. He had no shoes, no coat, and his clothes were soaked. I took off my glove and felt his neck. It was warm, a good sign. No hypothermia, not yet. He propped himself up on his hands and knees, and groaned.

"Let's get to your car," I said. "Where're your keys?"

"Pocket," he said. He'd begun to shiver, the shock and cold again. I took off my glove, said, "Excuse me," and reached into his jeans pocket. The keys were icy to the touch. "Let me put on my shoes," I said. "I can't walk with these skates." I sat down on the rock and moved my stiff fingers over the laces of the skates, moved slowly and frantically at the same time. Finally the shoes were on, and I left the skates where they lay. The man was still on his hands and knees. I bent over him, and with me lifting and a mighty effort, he stood up. "Let's go," I said.

We hobbled and stumbled up the dirt path, paused once or twice to catch our breath, and in a couple of minutes reached the car. It was parked next to mine. I walked him around to the passenger door, it was unlocked, and eased him into the front seat. Then I went around to the driver's side, climbed in, and started the car. "You got heat?" He didn't answer, just reached over to the dash and, with a trembling, gloved finger, pointed to a switch. "We'll let the car warm up for a minute. Give me your hands." I took off my glove and took his left hand in mine, removed the glove, and held the hand. It was beet red and cold, like a defrosting steak. I rubbed it, slowly, then moved to the other hand. I switched on the heat, and warm air blasted from the dash. The guy leaned into it.

"Take it easy, you'll be sitting here for a few minutes before you can move," I said.

"Jesus," the guy said, and his voice trembled. His face was in the heat.

"You've got to get out of those clothes," I said. "I got a blanket in my car. I always carry it. Take off those pants, you don't want to lose your legs."

80

"No, I'm fine," the guy said, shaky of voice. He stared straight ahead. "Soon as the car heats up."

"You don't want to lose those legs," I said. "It's your choice. I'll get the blanket."

I got out and got the blanket from my trunk. When I slid back to his car, he was in his underwear, the pants at his ankles. "My fingers don't work," he said, and he looked at me for the first time since I reached him at his splintered fishing hole. He eyed me as a man might eye a dentist or a cop, a potential incoming pain. There was a glint in the corner of his eye, a challenge. He looked like he hated something.

"I'll help," I said. So I helped him off with the jeans, then the shirt, then the T-shirt. I tossed his clothes in the back seat, put the blanket around his shoulders. "Keep this," I said.

We sat there for a minute in the blasting heat, kept our thoughts private. I expected him to say something, like, "Thanks," or something else. I couldn't help but think how lucky he was, out here on the ice at daybreak, in the water, with someone around to rescue him. But I didn't say that. Everything about his manner, about the way he stared at the dashboard, made it clear it wasn't time to talk.

"Got to go," he said, finally.

"Maybe I should take you to a hospital," I said.

"No," he said. "I'm okay."

"I don't know, you could be hurt."

"I said I'm okay," he snapped. "I don't need help."

He was angry with me. "It's your choice," I said.

His voice rose. "Look, I said I'm fine and I mean it, I'm goddamn perfect, all right?"

I looked for a sign in his eyes, but they weren't turned

my way. "Okay, then," I said. "Keep the blanket. Drive straight home, maybe take a warm bath."

"Yeah."

"Take a shot of something, whiskey, tea, whatever."

"Whatever."

He never looked at me again, never took his eyes off the dash.

"My name's Robert," I said. "Robert Silva. I live in town here."

"Torrington," he said, the next town over. He didn't mention his name.

"Well, okay," I said. "See you later, then. Stay off the ice." Neither of us laughed.

I decided against trying to shake hands. He didn't seem up for it, and our hands were a mess anyway. I got out of the car, shut the door, and gave a little wave through the window, but he stared at that dashboard. Minutes later I was gone, left him sitting there in his idling car, soaking up the warmth.

--

When I got home, Linda was in the kitchen, sipping coffee. Freddy was still asleep. I told her the story, about the guy at the pond, and remarked that it seemed odd he hadn't thanked me. Not that I needed it, and I didn't, but it just seemed odd to me.

"Maybe he was embarrassed by the whole thing," Linda said.

"He acted that way," I said.

"It's a guy thing. His manhood was threatened and all that," she said.

"He didn't even look my way much," I said. "He

looked more than embarrassed. He was angry, pissed off at me. He looked like he could hurt someone."

"Then it's true, he was embarrassed. He couldn't look you in the eye. You'd saved him from his own stupidity."

"The thing is, I never even thought that, that he was stupid. But now that you mention it, it was pretty stupid."

"Well, he'd also come close to death," she said. "That changes a person, at least for a moment."

"Could be. Whatever, it's over now. The guy's alive, and I feel pretty alive, too."

"That's right. You did your good deed for the day, for life even. You'll never have to worry again. Look at the bright side: You've bought salvation."

"If God was watching. Wonder if he gets up that early?"

A week later, I was in my trailer office at a construction site we were working, a strip mall down by the Hockanum River, and the kid who gets the mail popped his head in the door. "Got a package for you," he said. He held it up, a small box wrapped in brown paper. It was addressed to me through my company. There was no return address. I took out the scissors and opened the box, and wrapped in a newspaper were the skates, Freddy's skates, the ones I'd left at the pond. A sheet from a legal pad was folded, tucked into the side of the box. I opened it.

The note was written in pen. "You forgot your skates. You should give them to your boy when he grows up."

My heart turned cold. What in hell was the guy saying? But he couldn't know that Freddy was in a wheelchair. Or could he? Freddy's name was in the paper often enough, same last name as mine. I might even have been mentioned in an article or two. I put the skates back in the box, and put it on the floor next to my briefcase and had a long day at work.

Later that evening, while Freddy was in the sitting room running scales, I told Linda about the skates and the box.

"People," I said, "can do strange things."

"Men," she said.

"How's that?"

"Men do strange things. This is the way I see it: This guy failed, he did a stupid thing, and he put both of your lives in danger. He thinks, or at least vaguely feels, that he's less of a man for that one mistake. So he's got to top you, he's got to be the top dog. He's got to take your manhood down a notch. So what's the best way to chip away at a man? Chip away at his progeny, his son. By sending the box, he's saying that he knows you're no man either for the way your son turned out. You have a cripple for a son."

"You've got to be kidding."

"Either that, or the guy made an honest error and just sent back the skates, thought he was doing his own good deed for the day."

I thought about it, played detective for a moment. But first I had to ask. "You don't think I'm less of a man because of how Freddy turned out, do you?"

She exhaled, loudly, sipped some wine. "See, it's working, he's got you by the balls. Only a man would say something like that. I carried Freddy, for God's sake, for nine hellish months. He's my son, too. Don't you think that I wake up every morning wondering whether it was something I did? We're both part of Freddy, and I'm his mother."

"Sorry," I said.

"Besides," she said, "what's to say about how Freddy turned out? He's only ten, he hasn't turned out at all, not yet. But look at him. He plays the violin like an angel, he's got something to live for, he loves something. He has passion. He has more feeling than the two of us put together, except in his legs."

"I said I was sorry," and I was. "The point is, the guy would not have known I had a son, let alone a young son. I never told him about our family. He had to know from some other source, like a newspaper. And if that's how he found out, then he also knew Freddy was in a wheelchair. He did not make a mistake doing a good deed."

"So what are you going to do about it? It's men playing games, that's all. The guy's a loser. Leave it alone."

"Well, I've got to get rid of the skates."

And I did. I went out to the pond, early the next morning, with the skates. I sipped coffee, waited for some sun. When it broke over the trees, I strapped on the skates and pushed myself off from the shore, pumping left, then right, then left again as I picked up speed, let the wind soar around my face, let the tears flatten against my cheeks. I passed by the hole in the ice, frozen over once again. The box and fishing gear were gone. I didn't stop, just skated, leaned low, pushed into the wind and sun, pushed my legs, pumped my arms, listened to my breathing and the sound of a distant violin singing over the empty pond like a mother's call.

END

HIS SANITARY BED

I enter the revolving door and a large, flushed woman steps in behind me. She is unnerving, and her presence gives me the vague notion that this is going to be a difficult day. She is smoking a cigarette and that seems to be the key; she seems to have dense, willful purpose behind it, as if she'd rather burn through the door than do that little tiptoe geisha walk in its path. And so would I, but that's not the point. It is, after all, a revolving door.

Of course, in the time it takes to think this, the woman pushes too hard, I stumble, and my high heel snaps. Then she is gone before I can say a word. That confirms it. It is going to be a cliché sort of day.

I know that I will ask Brian, one of the office custodians, to take the shoe down to a repair shop at the corner. He will do it because he is the kind of man who would carry a woman's shoe and not feel odd about it. He would not do it for, say, Jane Limmers, our unpleasant office manager, who would frown at his doing personal favors for anyone, even middle-aged senior partners like me. But he will do it for me because he likes me, and that is because I like him.

Before I find Brian, I take off the other shoe and walk barefoot toward Jordan's office. I am having an affair with Jordan. In fact, the first time we heaved ourselves into each other's arms was here, in his office. It was insane.

It was insane because Jordan is younger than me, by fifteen years, and, more important, he has a wife. That is why I now call it an affair and not a relationship. The word itself is sullied, and that is how I have been feeling lately. In the beginning of an affair there are enticements; danger, passion, perhaps some small joys. At the very least, sex. That was the way it was with us. That, and maybe my need to feel desired again.

But toward the end of an affair—and they always end, don't they?—there is no future, no needful passion, no truth. It is hard to define which happens first, the end of it or the lies. One or the other or both of you looks deep into one or the other or both of your souls, and comes up lacking. Or comes up with a spouse.

I have met Jordan's wife, Freeda, only twice. The latest was yesterday when she came to the office to pick up their car. She needed to take it for servicing and then upstate with the children to visit her parents. She is a composed, bright woman, in some ways naive. But charming, always charming. She'd stopped by my office to inquire about my children and their health. I was nearly apoplectic with anxiety, but I held my own.

Freeda is the reason I no longer want this affair.

Maybe I never did, but who can tell about that? It happened. Not against my will, but I didn't have the energy to think about it at the time. I was exhausted, my husband was dead, and I was unhinged by the appeal of shallow excesses.

Besides—and this may be my touchstone—mistresses are pathetic people. Always waiting, always wanting. Always breathless. I don't like the image, I don't like the guilt and I don't want to continue to lose control. I have met the enemy and the enemy is me, etc. It is as simple as that.

Of course, we both have realized, even perhaps from the beginning, without saying so, that Jordan will not leave his wife. That is fine with me. I was never a thief of men, of husbands. I once had one and I don't want another, certainly not one that cheats on his wife. Luis, my husband, I am convinced never, ever cheated on me. As I never cheated on him. It was the one part of our contract that held. That, and the "until death do us part" bit.

Over the months I have learned that Jordan does not like to talk about Freeda. At times, when she and the kids are out of town, I visit him at his house in the suburbs. We will make dinner and heave ourselves into each other's arms, lately in a distracted sort of way, all over the house; on the couch, in the study, under the aquarium, even once on a toboggan in the garage. But never in their bedroom. We have never been in their bedroom. I once saw it when he was busy in the shower and it is clearly—I don't know, the *right* woman's bedroom. Freeda's perfume is everywhere and it is light, slightly fruity, sort of sweet. The thing is, the bedroom is hers and I simply cannot go that far.

—–

Jordan might be a genius. We are stockbrokers, and he is one of the best, at our firm or on the Street. I am also one of the best, and I have years of experience on him. We balance in that regard. It helps that he looks good, even great, and projects confidence as if he owns it. He can be reckless and so can I, our affair proves that, but he is equally calculating, both with other people's money and with his life. Jordan is, in many ways, without conscience.

Soon after Jordan joined our firm, my husband, Luis—Luis Miguel de Henriquez—became ill, then died, and it was not a good time for me or for our family.

The affair was much later. Now, walking barefoot toward his office, I am working out the details of ways to end it. I want to avoid clichés, but my intuition tells me that the experience with the broken shoe has defined the day. I am thinking this would work: "Jordan, I feel like a slut and you ought to as well but I know you don't, so I don't want us to heave ourselves, distractedly, at each other everywhere but the bedroom ever again."

His office is empty, but I know he is somewhere in the building. Jordan is nothing if not driven, and he is always early.

I turn and greet several secretaries by the coffee machine, and we joke about the broken shoe. Everyone is sympathetic to the revolving door problem. I ask if Mr. Baus, who is Jordan, is in yet and I get yeses and nods from all, but no other reactions. I periodically check to see if the office has picked up our trail. If they ever did, it would be disastrous. I would be mortified, at any rate. I have no background for this.

In my office, I find a note on my desk. It is on office memo paper and unsigned, typed, lying face down. It was not there last night. It says: "I know."

I quickly glance out my door to see if anyone is looking. They are all busy with their papers and shuffling this and that. No one has seen me. I crumple it, calm myself, and get to work.

—

My dead husband Luis betrayed his life with alcohol and regretted it too late. He wasn't a tragic drunk; he had no mystery, no air of the severe about him. He was, in the end, merely a resigned drunk.

Luis was Puerto Rican, born to a family of some note, a wealthy family with, Luis always said, ties to obscure Spanish aristocracy. His father's life consisted of running for public office and breeding polo horses on a large ranch in Arecibo, near San Juan. I met Luis in the '60s, while we were both students at Columbia. He was then a radical, albeit a privileged radical, an agitator for Puerto Rican independence. And a mesmerizing speaker. He was the first Puerto Rican I'd met who had blond hair and green eyes, and I was drawn to his voice, maybe to his accent. I was a fool for rolled "r's." In small groups we drank and talked, Luis using a mixture of clipped English and turgid Spanish, all the while flinging his arms about as if he were waving off bees.

"It is my dream, Cathleen," he would say, "to show you Puerto Rico." He rolled those "r's" like an idling motorboat. I loved him from the start.

Of course, Puerto Rican independence never came. After university, and after we married, Luis stayed in

New York to become a political correspondent for the *San Juan Star*. He wrote well, even very well. It was a good life then. It was good for many years.

Then, after the death of his father, Luis returned to Puerto Rico to deal with his mother and the family estate. Luis wanted to operate the ranch. His brothers wanted to sell, and they had arguments. The whole situation became central to his pride, and he ultimately lost. When he left Arecibo to return to me, he was deeply hurt.

Yet the sale of the Arecibo estate made Luis and his brothers wealthy men. He stopped writing for the *Star* but did not stop roiling in his bitterness, his failure. He invested money in other ranches, in other horses, and lost. He bought a small newspaper in upstate New York, and ran it so badly it folded. He couldn't even sell it. His money dwindled and his drinking became a problem; this is an old story. Luis had found the empty place all men fear.

Luis was a poor lover, often tired or incapacitated by the drink, but I never doubted that he loved me—and that is because I loved him—or needed me to help trim the frayed edges of his life. I supported him when he was drunk, when he lied to me. I watched it first as a wife, then as a spectator. I left him three times, but always came back to nurse him. Even when his body faltered, even when he was pathetic, his will was strong.

The end, a long time brewing, happened quickly. On a Monday Luis was playing basketball with Jimmy, our son, and on the Saturday of that week his heart exploded. His last words to me were whispered in his hospital room. He pulled me close. "I have always loved you," he said, "but I have corrupted it. I am so sorry."

Corrrupted, he'd said. He died later that night, while I slept in a chair next to his sanitary bed.

I see Jordan during the day but do not mention the note. I want to think about it a bit. It is an alarming development, but it just might work out for the better, if I use it well. It may be just what the doctor ordered.

Jordan must know eventually, I am sure of that, yet I see no reason to upset him at the office. When I first saw him in the hall he whispered, "You are glorious today." It sounded pointless and greasy, and I almost stopped to tell him so. But I passed. It passed.

Later he buzzes me and we arrange to meet at his home in the evening.

I arrive at the side door of his home and he meets me with a glass of champagne, standing in the shadows. Always a closet pragmatic, I say, "You need to open the garage so I can hide my car."

"Cathleen," Jordan says and he smiles a distant smile. He pulls me toward him and kisses me. Kissing Jordan is like taking the lid off a tin of coffee—it fills the air quickly, then evaporates just as quickly. I kick shut the door as it evaporates. As I've said, this is insane.

Two things will happen tonight. Freeda will call to say hello and Jordan will talk to her for a while. I will know she has said, "I love you," one or two times, because Jordan will answer, "Me too, honey," one or two times. He never says, "I love you" first, or at all. He never looks at me while he talks to Freeda—I usually leave the room—and he closes his eyes when he says, "Me too, honey."

The other thing that will happen tonight is I will tell Jordan about the note.

I have thought about it all day, and have reached no

conclusions. Maybe it is a prank, or maybe someone is just guessing about us. I cannot be sure that whoever left it knows anything. I cannot even be sure what the motive might be for letting me know that they know, apparently, about our affair. It is a mystery and that part worries me. Jordan will be deeply worried.

I finally tell him after the next bottle of wine is opened.

"Someone in the office might know about our affair," I say. I sense that I have spit out the word, as if it were a piece of spoiled meat. I feel like a hypocrite as I say it. Jordan is incredulous.

"What?" he asks.

"Someone left a note on my desk this morning. It said, 'I know.'"

"What do you mean, a note?"

"A note, a real note, not on e-mail, not a text, voice mail, whatever. Typed, on paper. That's all it said."

"It said, 'I know'?" he says. "Know what? What could they know?"

"What do you think?"

"Do you really think someone knows? What is this, a bad joke?"

"An educated guess would point to, yes, someone knows. I have nothing else to hide."

He shakes his head. "Good God. They can't know. It's impossible. No one can know. We've been discreet."

"Sharon knows."

"Sharon? How?"

"Jordan, I'm spending time away from home, and I have a good relationship with my daughter. I tell her where I'm going. I leave her an address in case there's an emergency."

"Are you telling me she knows about us?"

"She knows an address. She doesn't know you're married, if that's the issue."

"What about your son?"

"Jimmy is away at college."

"Well, the issue is that someone knows, someone in the office. Your daughter wouldn't call someone in the office, would she?"

Apparently I roll my eyes.

"Okay, okay, she wouldn't. Then it's someone in the office." He hesitates. "Why would they do this? Blackmail?"

A good point. It is something I've thought as well. I shrug my shoulders.

"I mean, I'm just covering the bases," he says. "What do we do?"

"Worry, is my guess." Then, "Maybe we should end this."

He looks at me, wide-eyed, pained. Suddenly—and this is of course the irony of clichés—I don't have the heart to follow through.

"Well," I say, "then let's be smart."

So we talk and worry together for a while. We decide to keep our eyes open and take things cautiously. The issue seems to be temporarily resolved, or at least postponed. We are both tired and I decide to go home. I leave him with his head in his hands.

The next night is the same. I go to Jordan's house, resolutely determined to follow through, and we eat, talk. No sex. We are distracted. Freeda calls, and they talk for close to an hour.

Later, Jordan is curious about my habits with Luis, this for the first time. He asks about our life together.

I tell him the truth. Luis is gone and our last memories were not good. What passion we had was truncated by his life, then his death, but he was not an evil man, just dangerous. In a way, he died happier than he should have. I am curious why Jordan asked.

"I wish I'd met him," he says.

"We should end this," I say.

"What?"

"Forget it," I say.

The next day passes and we are discreet at the office. Freeda comes by, her trip upstate was wonderful and she is going shopping. She talks with me for a while. I am sore with anxiety, it's almost physical. Freeda is guileless, a sweetheart. She reminds me of my daughter, and I feel like a sow. Finally, she goes to Jordan's office, and I don't see either of them for the rest of the day.

The next morning there is a note. An "I know" note. I call Jordan and tell him immediately, and he whispers, "This is getting serious, we have to think about things."

His voice is trembling.

"Who doesn't think about things?" I say.

––

Days go by, then the weekend. I spend it with Sharon and Jimmy, who has come down from college.

Jimmy, at the breakfast table: "So, Mom. Any guys barking at your door?"

Sharon: "Oh God, here it comes."

Jimmy: "It's just a question."

Me: "A tough question. Ask another one."

Jimmy: "Okay. How's your sex life?"

Sharon: "As if you could relate."

Jimmy: "Listen, Acne R Us, this is a conversation between two adults."

Sharon: "Correction, one adult and one mildly retarded adolescent."

Jimmy: "Mom, have I overstepped my bounds?"

Me: "Jimmy, I am your mother. Young men do not ask their mothers about their sex lives. Besides, I'm too old to have a sex life."

Jimmy: "These are modern times. Everyone has a sex life."

Me: "What are they teaching you at school? Am I paying for this?"

Jimmy: "Okay, okay. Really, how are things?"

Me: "I'm having some problems at the office. Nothing I can't handle."

Jimmy: "You look tired."

Me: "You wouldn't believe."

Later we order pizza and watch television. Jimmy is relaxed, charming, and his hazel eyes sparkle. He drinks a lot of beer. "Honey," I say. "I'm not one to count, but if I were one to count I'd say you've had four beers."

"Mom," he says. He is a little sloppy, a little high. "I'm in college. This is what we do."

"Jimmy Henriquez," I say. "Do you want guilt? I can do that for you."

Jimmy takes another pull on his beer, then sets it down. He smiles, slyly. "Would you have married him," he asks, "if he looked like a spic?"

"For God's sake," Sharon says.

I am not completely surprised. Luis called himself a spic, in jest. It was his sense of humor, self-deprecating and a little bit cagey. Jimmy isn't that cagey. And he's had too much to drink.

"You know," I say, "you are trying to be a snot and you are not succeeding. We had a good marriage, he was a good man, spic or no spic. You're a part of it."

Jimmy is quiet for a while. "You know what I think about?" he says, finally. "Can I be maudlin for a moment? He always smelled like eggnog."

"It was an aftershave. Old Bay Rhum."

Jimmy looks into his beer can. "You know, sometimes, like when I'm up there, up at school, I think how great it would be if he would show up. Say, for half an hour."

He stares at the TV, his father's son. His wet eyes reflect the white of the tube. In a moment, there are tears. Then tears in Sharon's eyes, and I go to Jimmy first and hold him. He puts his face on my chest, and sobs, and he is warm, as if he has a fever. I reach for Sharon and she drops to her knees, stretching to hug us both.

"Half an hour would hurt more," I say.

— —

Monday brings no news, but on Tuesday I come in to find a note. I confront Jordan with it, delivering it to his office. "I know," it says.

"Damn," Jordan says.

Later that day I find Brian, the office custodian, whom I trust and who, to the best of my knowledge, rarely seems to wallow in office gossip.

"Have you seen anything strange happening around here lately?" I ask.

He looks me straight in the eye and does an astonishing thing: he reaches out and touches my elbow.

"You mean in your office?" he asks.

"Yes," I say, "as a matter of fact."

"Well," he says. "Actually, I couldn't be all that sure."

I don't know what to make of this. Except that Brian is talking without malice and his eyes are clear.

"Try me, Brian."

"Yes, ma'am."

"What about my office?"

Brian clears his throat. "You know, it's not like it's any of my business."

"Brian," I say slowly, deliberately, as if—I hate to admit this now—as if I were talking to a schoolboy. "Have you seen someone going into my office?"

His eyes flicker, searching for a way to tell his tale. He discovers it. "During regular hours?" he asks.

"No. Late at night. Or early," I say, "before I come in. Am I right?"

"Well," he says, struggling, "I'd guess that's right."

"Help me out here, Brian," I say. "Who comes in early?"

But, of course, I have the answer at the precise moment the words leave my mouth.

"Good Jesus," I say.

Brian thinks about it for a moment, getting his bearings. "Anyway, ma'am," he says. "How's that shoe doing?"

—–

The day passes and Jordan is distant. The next day another "I know" note has turned up at my desk. It is in the same style as the others, on office memo paper, typed, and unsigned. It all seems so incredible to me, but I have been feeling light, as light as an ash over fire. I am being delivered.

Before I have the chance to do it, Jordan, my married man, calls me on the office phone.

"We have to talk," he whispers.

"Absolutely. When?"

"Are you okay? You sound funny."

"I'm hilarious," I say. "When do we talk?"

"We can go to lunch."

I meet him at Dominick's, a small, dark diner across town. Jordan has already had a drink by the time I arrive. I decide to have a drink as well. Within minutes I decide against lunch. We just banter and sip, avoiding the notes issue for a while. His face is drawn and the lines are deep. Jordan has rarely looked so handsome, and I am almost overcome with his discomfort. Almost, but not quite. The thing is, I am in a good mood. This damn great mood. So I decide to let him do all the work.

"About these notes," he says, finally.

"Yes, the notes. Brilliant," I say. "Cowardly, of course, but brilliant. Saves us both a lot of pain."

"What? What's brilliant about them? It's a bad situation."

"You bet," I say. I realize my voice has registered enthusiasm, like a cheerleader.

He fixes his dark eyes on me. "No, it's a real problem."

"It is, and you know what you want to do. You want to break it off. Am I right?"

He sits up, slightly. "Shouldn't we think about it?"

"Think about what? I'm confused. I thought it's been thunk."

"Pardon? No, I mean, do you love me? That's the first question."

I am struck by his question. It doesn't fit. The introduction of it at this point is perverse.

"What's love got to do with it?" I say. Unfortunately, I get a kick out of that.

He stares at me, squinting.

"It's a song, and a movie," I say, and I laugh some more. "Think Tina Turner."

Jordan fiddles with his glass. He is peeved. "I guess I shouldn't have been so personal."

"Look, this doesn't make sense," I say. "You want to end this and I want to end this. We're dancing around it. Why?" I feel as if I've had about eight drinks.

"You want to end it?" he says. "Why?"

"Hold on," I say. "Let's get back to the original game plan. It's the notes. Stick with the notes."

"Well, yes," he says. "Okay, someone knows about us." He hesitates again. "Do you really want to break it off?"

"Jordan, forget about love. Freeda loves you, that's all you need to know."

"I know she loves me. I just didn't know that you wanted to break it off."

"Wait, am I the one who left the notes on my desk? Remember the notes, Jordan, concentrate on the notes."

"Okay, okay, already. Someone knows. Maybe we have to call it quits. I'm just surprised that you—"

"That's right," I interrupt. "Call it quits. Finito. End of the chapter." I begin to like these euphemisms. "The last waltz. Lower the sails, turn out the lights."

He is struggling. "The last waltz?"

"Let's let sleeping dogs lie and—what is it?—piss on the fire. I can't believe I know that. Look, you have a life—it's a good life . . . and so do I. So let's call it a day. It's a wrap."

He stares, gaping like a guppy in a fishbowl.

101

"Last down and goal?" I say, "The cards are on the table? End of the highway?"

"Uhm," he says.

"Curtains," I say. I am in this damn fine mood.

"You are making light of this," he says.

"The fat lady is singing."

"Jesus."

"You know," I say. "We could have had this conversation months ago. Actually, no, it's my fault. I should have had this conversation months ago."

"But the notes just started coming around."

"Oh, that's right," I say. "Of course. The notes just started coming around. What more do you want to hear about them?"

He squints hard, switches gears, almost audibly. Jordan, I realize, has always been easy to read. "Anyway," he says, "you're sure you want to do this?"

"Look, it's done, it's de facto. You're doing the right thing, don't stop now. And we can't remain friends, by the way. We're professionals."

"Look," he says, "I don't mean we should break it off forever. Maybe just for now."

"No," I say. "We will break it off forever. We're both too weak for this sort of thing. Much too weak." Then I push back my chair, gather my things, and walk.

We go separately, discreetly, back to the office, and I am in the lobby before I notice the revolving doors thumping behind me, shushing and soft.

Later Jordan calls me at my desk. "Just checking in," he says.

Then I have this urge, this sudden urge, to call Freeda to tell her how much I've always admired her and liked her, and to let her know that I'm happy and my kids are fine and how are hers and that forging binding love, binding anything, is desperate and heroic and wholly possible.

But I know I won't call; I've had it with clichés.

"Cathleen?" Jordan says.

Except for the one where I hang up, gently.

END

BLUE JAYS

The pond was still, save for the lone rower. He pulled hard at the oars in a determined way, as if he had a destination in mind, as if he had a purpose, and the boy on the shore heard the occasional grunt as he strained. The oars thumped in their gunwales and the rower nicked the water occasionally, sending streams across the stern.

"Bet he wishes he had a little motor right now," the boy's father said quietly. He thought for a moment. "At least he's got a boat."

"It's okay without a boat," Kevin said.

"Sure it is." Winking. The father was, among other things, a championship winker. "Thanks anyway, Kev."

"Sure," Kevin said, but he knew it. Of course his father wished they had a boat. Wished for a bigger house, for the money to take a real vacation once in a while. Even just a car newer than the '65 Suburban parked up by the road, now ten years old. He wished for a lot of things, and Kevin did, too, because, and he knew this by instinct, if his father ever got his wishes, those winks would have come from a different place.

Their lines were in the water, bobbers drifting. In the half hour they'd been standing at their spot, the spot they came to or tried to come to most every weekend in summer, they hadn't had a bite. "Fish are closer to shore this time of day anyway," Kevin said.

"Could be," his father said. "Could be at that. We'll see. Maybe a largemouth tonight."

The rower approached, indirectly, skewed to the west a bit. Kevin looked up and his father had begun to frown in that way he did.

"Isn't he kind of close?" Kevin said.

"He is. Whole lot of lake to fish on, not a soul in sight, and here we all are." His father exhaled.

The rower, his back to them, let go of the oars and they dangled in the water. He was thin, skin the color of a brown paper bag. He turned and smiled, then raised an arm in sort of salute. He held a pint bottle in his hand, took a pull from it, and wiped his mouth with his hand. The father frowned just a bit harder—Kevin sensed it without even looking at him—not because he was a priss or anything like that. He was the type of guy who'd bring a few cold beers on a fishing trip himself. He just wasn't the type of guy who'd salute a man and his kid with one.

"Any luck?" the rower shouted across the hollow water. Smiling.

"Of course," Kevin's father mumbled, to no one in particular. Then, to the rower, "No. Not yet. You?"

"Oh, feeling lucky now," the man said. His words were thick. "Oh yeah. This looks like the spot."

The rowboat was maybe thirty-five yards from shore. "Dad," Kevin said, "this is our spot."

"Yes, it is," he said. "And we just told him we haven't caught a thing here. What's he think, we're lying?" It was the greater offense. Not that the man was crowding them in a spot they'd found first, but that he was, implicitly, accusing them of dishonesty.

The man grabbed his pole, which was propped up on the stern, and stood, unsteady. He already had some kind of lure on the line, and cast it toward the center of the lake, reeling in as soon as it hit the water. "C'mon baby!" he said, loud enough for them to hear.

"'C'mon baby'?" Kevin said. "Who says 'C'mon baby'?"

"This can't be good," his father said.

The rower finished reeling and dropped his pole, clattering, to the bottom of the boat. He leaned down and picked up his bottle from somewhere, then stood back up, rocking the boat, and unscrewed the top. He took another sloppy pull, drained it. He shook the bottle, as if shaking it would magically make some more appear. But it somehow stayed empty. And he tossed it overboard. Then, as an afterthought, he tossed over the screw top.

"Jesus," the father whispered.

The guy turned as if he'd heard, but grinned, a wide drunk's grin, out of place and loopy. When he bent over to grab his pole, he pitched sideways and—in Kevin's mind's eye it would always be in slow motion, almost graceful—he went straight over the side of the boat.

Maybe his shins grazed the side as he fell, but other than that, he made almost no sound. He cut the water with a tiny splash, perfect, like an Olympic diver, and disappeared.

Kevin held his breath for a second, and when the guy didn't come up he said, "Dad, he's down."

But his father was already in motion, his pole on the ground, boots and T-shirt coming off. In seconds he was waist-deep in the water, and he turned over his shoulder. "Stay there Kevin, don't move." Then he was swimming, a fast crawl, his arms slapping the water like the flats of oars.

––

Kevin dropped his rod, frozen to the mucky bank, as his father grunted and plowed the water. Finally his father was at the side of the boat. He stopped, and, treading, peered down through the copper water. Kevin could tell he was feeling around with his feet. He jackknifed, his backside suddenly in the air, and dove, his legs and toes straightening, and slipped into the gurgle.

In seconds the father was back up, spluttering water, moving away from the spot. "He's stuck!" he shouted, maybe to Kevin, maybe to himself. "Belt's on a branch." He hesitated for a moment, then turned to his son. Across the water Kevin could see the eyes knitted together, the frown, the hesitancy. A man and a decision.

His father sucked in a great breath and jackknifed again, another perfect dive in an afternoon full of them. But when he didn't come up immediately, Kevin took two or three steps into the water. The water by the rowboat began to purl softly. "Dad!" Kevin shouted. Then it churned. "Dad! Get out!" The boat rocked in the tiny waves. "Dad?"

Suddenly his father's toes breached the surface, thrashing, and Kevin was in the lake, bolting toward him. He kept his head above water so he could fix his eyes on where they were. Where the boiling water was.

He swam like a madman, every second and every breath thundering, his arms aching from the speed of churning. As he glimpsed the water ahead, at the rowboat, it began to go still, and by the time he got to the boat, tiny waves soughed against the rowboat's hull. "Jesus," he heaved. "Jesus Christ."

He grabbed a great breath, and plunged his head under, and he wasn't nearly prepared for it. Nothing in his life could have prepared him for it. They were both directly beneath, softly waving with the currents in a slow motion dance, shafts of amber sunlight flickering around their arms and legs. The rower was upright, his arms floating, lolling above his head as if reaching for an apple in a tree. Kevin could almost touch the man's hands with the bottoms of his sneakers. The fisherman's belt was hooked on the branch of an underwater tree trunk. His eyes were wide open, frozen in shock.

His father was face down on the bottom, a couple of feet from the rower, his arms perfectly positioned under his head. A man taking a quiet nap.

The empty pint bottle glistened in the sun, a couple of feet from the rower.

The boy screamed, still underwater, and came up sputtering and grabbed the boat, seized by a panic he'd never in his waking moments known. "Jesus," he shouted to the air. "Move!" He plunged his head back into the silence. His father hadn't heard. Hadn't moved.

Kevin went back up, then pushed off the boat and dove, pulling himself down. He touched his father's back, it was warm, and tried to grab his arms. They were slick and he lost his grip. He went back up, sucked in another breath, and dove again. This time he grabbed the waist of his father's shorts, and as the man budged his head rolled sideways in an exaggerated, violent motion. Kevin yelped again, swallowed water again, and dropped him. His father settled to the bottom and slow puffs of sand muddied the water around him.

Kevin tried again, and again, but couldn't move him and finally, exhausted, surfaced and hung on to the side of the boat and shouted, "Help us!" He shouted it again, and his tears mixed with the lake water until his face was hot and he gagged on his snot and his arms started to give, and he began to slip.

"Can't somebody please help us please," he whispered to the boat.

—-

The details of the days following were as murky as the water his father drowned in—or, more accurately, the water in which the panicked rower had grabbed and snapped his neck.

The wake was relentlessly miserable, for everyone. The combination of the preternatural wailing from his mother's Italian side of the family and the blank incredulousness from his father's Irish Southie relatives filled the funeral home room with a distorted, imprecise energy. Kevin's mother, Mary, had finished most of her crying by then and spent her time in line with her arm around Colleen, who hadn't completely grasped the situation, even with her father lying there in the open coffin. Still taking that nap. Kevin had refused point blank to kneel at it and say a prayer, but he did thank God that his mother had let it go at that. Maybe she was too worn down by her grief to insist on it, or maybe she just understood. He glanced at his father once or twice, but quickly looked away because his chest wasn't rising up and down, and every time it didn't, just when Kevin thought it should, had to, it took his own breath away. He was vaguely aware that they were in Franklin O'Keefe's Funeral Home and that flowers covered the walls and floor around snuffing people kneeling at a coffin in the front of the room, but that, he told himself with decreasing assurance, wasn't his dad over there. It was a dummy in a cop's uniform, a lurid likeness and a bad one at that. He felt mildly sedated by the whole thing.

"So young," Aunt Rita said as she got to him in line and caressed his cheek with a trembling, cool hand. He had no idea if she was talking about him, or his father.

"Did your best," Uncle Colin said as he bent over and gave Kevin a crushing bear hug. The boy caught the Scotch on his uncle's breath, a sweet, humid cloud and it made him want more. "You're a hero, you know that?"

"Sure," Kevin said.

Colin blinked, as if to clear his head, and put his hand on Kevin's shoulder. "I know," he said. He leaned in. "Least the nigger's dead, too."

"Colin!" Rita said, and smacked him on the arm.

"I'm just tryin'—" he looked back and leaned in again, a conspirator. "Look, Kevin, you're a man now, nearly. You know what I'm talking about. What's the lesson here?"

"Colin!" Rita said, and grabbed his arm this time, pulled at him.

"You listen to what I say, Kev."

"It wasn't like that."

Uncle Colin blinked again. "Like what?"

"Like that," Kevin said. "I mean, I never heard him call someone a nigger." He shocked himself by saying it, out loud like that. He locked onto his uncle's eyes and saw the flash, the bloodlust the word carried. Colin was his father's younger brother by three years, a massive train wreck of a man with broad shoulders and a red, fatty face framed by bushy yellow eyebrows that arched nearly vertical when he laughed. But he wasn't laughing.

"Maybe, Kevin." Colin breathed thickly. "Maybe not. Maybe he was a saint. But look where it got him."

Rita started to pull him away and Mary leaned over, hissed, "Colin, you leave that boy alone." Like a cat ready to pounce.

"Just telling it like it is, Mary," he mumbled over his shoulder as he drifted into the crowd. "I loved him, too, you know."

Later, at the house after the funeral, it would be more of the same. Among the salad plates and rolls and trays of lasagna brought over by the Italian side, there would be small groups of men, laughing a bit, then going quiet, dark and brooding. They'd begin to whisper, their faces red, fingers jabbing the air and each other's chests. Thick fingers around shot glasses. They'd glance at Kevin and Colleen once in a while and fix them with strained smiles mixed with pity and a bit of shame, then turn back to each other with eyes on fire. The Italian side would begin to mix with the Irish side, the drinks would flow, and later that night a nondescript car, license plate removed, would roll slowly down a street in Dorchester or Roxbury. It would be filled with white men and baseball bats. Some would be carrying box cutters, maybe a bicycle chain or two. And the first black man they saw, the first "look at that *fucking* nigger acting like he owns the street" they saw, age more or less unimportant, they'd jump him and leave him broken and flayed in a seeping pool on the sidewalk. And if he died, fine. It was an eye for an eye, a biblical retribution, one more step toward salvation. They'd go home and clean up, and later celebrate in a neighborhood bar, the world once more in balance. It would probably go unreported, but if it was, the investigation would go nowhere. The police would quietly drop it within weeks after hearing the whispers out of Southie: "It was about the Matt Mahoney thing." And the blacks in the slums would know enough to let it go away until, a few weeks later, a group of young men would take up bats and zip guns and climb into a car and cruise the outskirts of Southie.

It was the marrow of life in his part of the world, imbedded in the language of that life. The spades, niggers, shines were on one side in the slums of Dorchester and Roxbury, and the micks circled the wagons in Dorchester, in next-door South Boston, and on the other side of the Mystic in Chelsea, Revere, Charlestown, and over up in Somerville. The dagos, wops, guidos hunkered down in the North End, and scattered around the city to run their restaurants and delis. The chinks, dinks, slants commandeered a couple of blocks of downtown, Chinatown, between Atlantic Avenue and the theatre district that butted up against the Combat Zone, a red light district filled with haggard prostitutes, adult bookstores, and strip joints. The brahmins, bluebloods, assholes holed up in Back Bay and Beacon Hill, and in the suburbs of Cambridge and Newton and Brookline, pretending the city was still theirs, refusing to believe that the turf violence they read about in the morning papers had anything to do with them; it might have happened in another country for all they knew or cared. To them it was all about the city's trailer trash slugging it out like drunks at a county fair. It was about people who weren't them and would never be them.

But to the men and women in Kevin's neighborhood, skin was an elemental fact of life. Fact one: a black face was not welcome here, and a white face in Roxbury was always behind a cop's uniform or under a fireman's helmet. Fact two: it's not about prejudice, it's about family, protecting our families is all. Fact three: It's always going to be this way, as long as the spades act like the spades they are.

The rower also had a funeral. Two days before his dad's wake and funeral, Kevin had read the obit in the paper under "Emmanuel Gonsalves, 29, master carpenter and avid fisherman." It was an irony he kept to himself—his mother and Colleen wouldn't have understood it, and in another situation it would have been a hoot. Avid fisherman my ass, he thought. Avid drunk, or avid destroyer-of-lives. He'd allowed himself to think— despite his defense of his father, despite Colin—he'd thought: "Avid nigger."

The other obit ran the same day, the same page, which, Kevin was sure, his Uncle Colin saw as an insult. It said: "Matthew Mahoney, 38, police sergeant, leaves family in South Boston."

That same day, the paper had run a page-two follow-up about the deaths: "Coroner on Deaths of

Fisherman and Hero Cop: Accidental," and his mother cut it out and her tears stained it as she filed it in a scrapbook next to the other articles, under the obituary.

Cops from all over New England gathered at the funeral, all in full formal dress with white gloves, some with swords, others with rifles, and one in a kilt, with bagpipes, which he played quietly but purposefully over to the side while Father Bannon said the service. The coffin was draped with an American flag, and they presented the folded flag to Mary, who was sitting on a chair under her black veil. She handed it to Kevin, and he held it until they got home, thought about holding it for the rest of his life. And when all was said and done, when all the pomp and sword raising and rifle salutes were over, and as they filed toward the limo that would take them home, all he could think was that Gonsalves's funeral most likely was, ultimately, not much different. In the end, despite the heavy flag he held in his hands, it's someone's father in a box in the ground. A dark place.

After the gathering at the house, and after the men had filed out with hugs and whiskey on their breaths and hands beginning to clench and flex as if already reaching for the bats, it was just Mary and her sister Anna, and Kevin and Colleen. The women drank coffee, Kevin sipped pop, and it finally dawned on him, it hit him cold and hard in the back, like how he imagined the blade of a knife might feel, that this was it, this was the way it would be for the duration. Alone at home. No fishing, no Fenway franks, no thick aftershave, no more Mom and Dad laughing in the kitchen trying to disco dance like they'd done last week. No more any goddamn thing.

"Kevin," Mary said from her seat on the couch, and he looked at her for the first time in days. Her plain, black dress, buttoned from neck to hem, nearly reached her ankles, and her black knit sweater had slipped back over her birdlike shoulders, probably from all the hugging. Her wavy hair, also jet black, had been brushed a hundred times by Aunt Anna the night before the funeral, then parted on the left. Her alabaster face was set off by wide, light brown eyes the color of a Bit-o-Honey. She'd never looked more sweet to him, and Kevin, for the first time, glimpsed the power of anguish. Grief can make a person beautiful, it really can.

"Kevin," she said, "you were wonderful today, honey. I'm so proud of you." She turned to his sister, who was sitting on Aunt Anna's lap. "And you, too, Colleen, you were such a big girl. You're the best, both of you, the best a mother could want." She gestured and they both went to her arms, and she wrapped them in perfume. Her face was warm and damp.

"So, why don't you two brush your teeth and run off to bed," she said, and held them out and sniffed. "Aunt Anna and I have a few things to talk about, okay?"

"But Mom—" Colleen said.

"I'll come in a minute and read a story," Mary said. "Scoot."

Kevin said goodnight to Anna and turned, and his mother said, "Kevin, wait a sec, would you? Colleen, you brush first, Kevin will catch up." Colleen left, and Mary cleared her throat.

"Kev. You've had it roughest of all."

"You, too."

"Well, it hasn't been good," she said, but he knew, he could see it in her wide eyes. She was thinking: *But I wasn't there. You were.* "And it'll probably get worse in a while."

"It can't get worse, Mom. How?"

She stared for a moment, her Bit-o-Honey eyes moist with fatigue. She was thirty-three years old, the prettiest woman in the world, a widow with two kids. And instantly he knew it could get worse.

"Kev, about Uncle Colin," she said.

"I've heard it before."

"I know. I know. You have to understand that he loved your father very much, he was his younger brother, like Colleen and you. He's maybe just a bit frustrated."

Just a bit. And some guy in the 'Bury is finding out about that right now.

"But the most important thing to remember," she said, "to remember about your father, is that he wasn't an angry man. He didn't lead an angry life. That's why he wasn't like some of your uncles."

"And some of the aunts," Anna interjected.

"Yes, sure, some of the aunts. Anna, would you look after Colleen for a minute, please?"

Aunt Anna cleared her throat, then nodded slowly. She stood up and caressed Kevin's head on the way out.

"Do you understand, Kev?"

He did, but despite that, it rose up in him and he let it go because it was time. "But a Negro killed him. A drunk black guy, right? What are people *supposed* to say?" He realized he was raising his voice.

"People can say whatever they want. But I'm talking about you, Kevin. You can still learn from him. From your father."

"Learn what?" he said. Sneered, really, though he hadn't wanted to. What he really wanted was to bolt from the room because he knew goddamn well what she was talking about, and he also knew that he wanted to be angry. He would've enjoyed the hell out of being angry. He wanted to be angry at Colin for being stupid, to be angry at the Negro for killing his father, to be angry at his mother for asking him not to be angry. But most of all, he wanted to be angry at his father for dying before he got to him.

"Just, Kev," she said softly, and her eyes warmed again. "Your father wasn't perfect, but he never let bitterness take over his life."

"So?"

"So that allowed him to do the right thing. Like that day. He was doing the right thing."

"And that's good? That's his reward? Do the right thing until death do us part?"

She sucked in a breath, then whispered, "That's not fair."

"No, it's *not* fair!" he shouted. He began to shake and he tried to stop and hated himself for not being able to. Again, like at the boat. Great big gobs of air and acrid salt.

"Come here, baby," Mary said.

He walked over and knelt in front of her, and she put her arms around him, stroked his back, whispered in his ear. "You did the right thing, too, Kevin. See?" and she kissed his ear. "Just don't let this anger build, and you'll always know what to do."

He sobbed, his voice muffled by her sweater. "What do you mean?"

She hesitated, then whispered, "You'll know."

They held each other for a minute, rocking, and she said, "We're going to miss him terribly, I'm afraid."

Kevin picked up his head, searched her eyes for more tears, but there were none. "I just wish he'd come back one more time," he said. "Just for a while. Just so I could tell him some things."

"He knows," she whispered.

—-

Sometime around the beginning of August, he began to shoot the birds. He had no reason for it, no explanation. Hadn't even asked himself what it might be like to shoot a bird. He hadn't wondered what it was that drove him to pick up the gun and pull the trigger. When it came down to it, to the moment, it was just a thing to do. He was in his room the first day, idling, when his eye caught the dull barrel of his Daisy pellet gun in the corner of his room. And he picked it up, hefted it, and looked out the window. Sighted it. And that was that, as banal an act as he could have summoned.

It lasted only three days, and in the end his spree tallied two blue jays, a crow, and a wounded cat. In the end, the guilt and the act caught up with him, and he'd sickened himself when the last jay dropped fluttering and trilling from its perch at the feeder. He'd watched the struggling bird hit the ground, and his eyes welled up and he stepped back and sat on the edge of his bed, tired, tired as though he'd never been tired before.

At first, as he told the old ladies later, it was a lark, no pun intended, which he instantly regretted. They hadn't thought it funny, but looked at him blankly, eyes questioning, not like he was evil or a madman , but as if he were the kind of person they'd never have expected to do something like that.

"We'd never have expected you, of all people Kevin Mahoney, to do something like this," Miss Agatha Doyle said, creakily. They were in the kitchen of the ancient sisters' house.

"No," Miss Betty Doyle added, blinking like a bird herself, "not in a million years, not young Kevin."

"Yes, a lark, a lark indeed," Miss Agatha said softly. The corners of her mouth turned up slightly, as if she were trying out a smile that didn't quite fit. "Well, it all begs for an answer, doesn't it?"

Faced with it, with the truth of the two sisters in their bright, spotless kitchen and a kettle on the boil and the faint smell of sour milk and not a sign of a man anywhere, ever, his brow went cold. Not that he hadn't nearly puked the last time he'd pulled the trigger, but facing them here, in their house, the feeder swaying gently in the breeze of their sparse backyard, the bile rose in his gut.

"But first a bit of tea," Miss Betty said brightly. "Sugar and cream, Kevin?"

"Sure," he said, "thanks." He'd never had a cup of tea in his life. The thought occurred to him that the sisters, who had no children, who'd never married as far as he knew, probably hadn't had a bottle of pop in their house since they were kids growing up in it.

Miss Betty bounced from the table and made her way to the counter to fix the tea. A grey cat darted through the hallway by the kitchen, and another, an orange and grey tabby Kevin recognized as if he were sighting it again, slid up against Miss Agatha's leg, and she stroked its head.

"I believe you've met Basil," she said to Kevin, her eyes twinkling. She rhymed the name with "dazzle."

"Oh, they've met," Miss Betty, by the counter, said. Her voice was light, as if she were about to deliver the punch line to a joke, and in fact she began to cackle. "Of course they've met. Young Kevin *shot* Basil, don't you remember?"

"Oh, I remember," Miss Agatha said, and she laughed as well. Her long, translucent fingers worked their way lightly around the cat's head.

Miss Betty brought the tray to the table and put a cup in front of each of them. She stood, pouring, as Miss Agatha's bright eyes darted between him and the cat. He stirred his cup slowly, the same way he'd seen his mother and father stir their coffee. Then he took a deep breath.

"Did I hurt her?" he said. "I mean, I didn't want to. I'm a moron."

"He, dear," Miss Agatha said. "Basil is a boy."

"Fixed, of course," Miss Betty said, and Kevin noted a flush rising to her cheeks. "I mean, it wouldn't do to have too many cats in the house, would it?"

"Wouldn't," Miss Agatha said. "Wouldn't at all." She sipped her tea and gently pushed a plate of Lorna Doones toward him.

"No, thanks," he said. He hadn't sipped his tea, either.

"By the way," Miss Agatha said. "We haven't talked to your mother about this. Are you worried? Well, don't fret, we haven't talked to your mother at all."

He had been worried of course, all day long. Not for fear of getting in trouble, but for fear of seeing his mother cry again. The day had started early in the morning, about five-thirty, as he'd circled the neighborhood delivering newspapers. Normally most everyone was asleep, and certainly the sisters were always asleep at that hour. But this morning the lights had been on in the Doyle house, and Miss Betty had stepped out just as he'd walked up their stoop with the *Globe*. "Kevin," Miss Betty had said, "how are you?"

He'd been startled by her sudden appearance, but she was fully dressed in a light summer shift and makeup, her wispy blue hair perfectly combed. He'd known instantly what was in store.

"Money's not due 'til Friday, Miss Betty," he'd said, panicked.

"Oh, I know that."

"Oh."

"Kevin, dear. Would you do Miss Agatha and I the honor of coming by for tea today? Say, about three-thirty?"

He'd stared, sinking. "Sure," was all he could say.

"We have a secret!" she said, and giggled.

He'd stood on the steps, unable to move. If he could have, he knew he would have run.

She'd taken a step down the stoop and leaned over, close. He could smell the fruity perfume hovering above her chest. She'd whispered, "It's about the birds, dear."

Then she'd stood up and ruffled his head, and said in a cheery voice. "Run along or you'll be late for a glorious summer day! And don't forget our date!" She'd turned and walked back into the house.

--

Now they were at the table, his tea untouched, Kevin waiting for the hammer to come down. He deserved it, he knew that. He had no explanation for anything. In the end there had been no epiphany about shooting the birds, no moment of truth. Just him on the edge of a bed, empty and guilty.

"No," Miss Betty said. "No need to talk to your mother about this, lovely woman. No need at all."

"Because it's you," Miss Agatha said, "just you we'd like to talk to." She scratched Basil's head with one hand, brought a Lorna Doone to her thin lips with the other. "Just one thing, though. Little Colleen wasn't involved, was she." It wasn't a question, it was a statement.

"No," Kevin said, shouted almost. "Not at all. Just me. It's me, that's all."

"Good," Miss Betty said. "We knew. We just wanted to hear it from your lips."

Miss Agatha brushed off Basil, who shook his head and, seeing no treats falling from above, padded out of the kitchen. Miss Agatha sipped her tea. "So tell us about it, Kevin."

He didn't know what to say, so he let the first thing that came to mind slide out. "I just did it."

"Well, yes, I expect so," Miss Agatha said. She turned to her sister. "But we think we know why you did it, don't we Betty? We know."

"We certainly do," Miss Betty said, and she clapped her hands together in the manner of a child who wants to be called on in class. "It's because he's angry. Angry as a bedbug."

"No, that's *crazy* as a bedbug, dear," Miss Agatha said. "But that's not what you meant to say, is it?"

"Oh, I suppose not," Miss Betty said, her eyebrows knitted. "Our Kevin isn't crazy, is he? He's angry, I'm almost positive of that."

"Yes, dear, Kevin is angry. Say, angry as a fly on tar paper."

"Oh, I'm not sure I like that one, Agatha. I don't know if Kevin should be compared to a fly. After all, he's a young boy, and a bright, beautiful boy at that. Albeit one who shot our cat."

"I really didn't mean to," Kevin said. "I mean, I was shooting at a crow. I missed."

Miss Agatha continued on as if Kevin hadn't just offered his first real explanation of the Basil caper.

"I see your point, Betty," she said. "Yes, flies are rather squalid, aren't they. Why don't you say, angry as a bag of bees?"

"Oh, of course. Lovely! Bees *are* angry, or at least they seem to be. I mean, they certainly would be if they were in a bag, I should think. Yes, I like that one. You know, though, I was just wondering. What is it about bedbugs that makes them crazy? Or, are they crazy, after all? I mean—"

"I am," Kevin said, and he realized, a bit too loudly. "Angry, I mean. Sometimes. But still, I shouldn't have shot the birds. I mean it, I'm sorry. I'm an idiot."

They both turned to him and blinked, rapidly, almost in unison.

"Oh," Miss Agatha said, as if Kevin had just walked into the room. "Yes, let's get on with it. Now, where were we?"

"Kevin is angry," Miss Betty said.

"Oh, yes. Angry as a bag of bees. Now, Kevin, you must have known, sitting up there with your rifle, that you wouldn't be able to shoot into our backyard indefinitely. Without getting caught."

"I'd stopped," Kevin said. "After a few days, it was."

"Well of course you did, you poor dear," Miss Betty said, and her face turned down, betraying pity, or maybe, Kevin thought, a gas attack.

"We saw you," Miss Agatha said. "Heard it the first

time, then found the dead blue jay. But when Basil came in with a bruise on his haunch—it was bleeding a bit actually—we began to watch."

"Then eventually we saw you *pop* those two other birds," Miss Betty said, clapping her hands again.

"Yes we did," Miss Agatha said. "Your little rifle sticking out the second floor window. Your bedroom, I'd guess, isn't it?"

"Yes," Kevin said.

"Pop! Pop!" Miss Betty exclaimed, her face a sea of joy.

"Indeed," Miss Agatha said. "And after the last bird, well, that's when we decided to have this chat with you. Just the three of us, and here we are."

"All cozy as bugs in a rug," Miss Betty said, "with our tea and—oh! Bugs again!"

"Not to worry, Betty, dearest," Miss Agatha said, "we're all friends here. But I think our friend Kevin is more than angry, though, isn't he. Aren't you Kevin? Something more, I think. Tell us about it."

He wasn't sure what she was saying, and he was tired. He shrugged.

"She means, Kevin," Miss Betty said, "that there is something more. Something about what happened, isn't that it, Agatha?"

"Yes, it is," Miss Agatha said. "Far be it for us to bring it up, Kevin, all over again, but I think there's some more you want to say, to get it out, as the young people are saying these days. I think you're more than angry. You're sad, enormously sad. You have a right to that."

"Of course," Miss Betty said. "Terribly unhappy I would think."

"What we mean, Kevin," Miss Agatha said, "is that

125

you tried your best. That day. But it didn't work. And you're still angry and sad about it."

"You feel as if your worth has diminished," Miss Betty said.

"Exactly. And you're—"

"A coward," Kevin said, and he surprised himself when he said it. Out loud, like that.

"No, no," Miss Betty said. "Not that at all. You're a brave young man, the bravest."

"No," he said. "It's a big lie."

"Well!" Miss Betty said. "Did you hear, Agatha? He thinks he's a coward, but he most definitely is *not!* Not in the very least! Oh, look what we've done!"

"Kevin," Miss Agatha said. "Put that out of your head immediately. You did what you could do. I had intended to say that you were *bullying* yourself."

"No," he said, gathering himself. "I am a coward. I shot the birds."

"And Basil, too," Miss Betty said pleasantly, as if she were reminding him about another item for the shopping list.

"Of course you shot the birds, dear," Miss Agatha said. "But ultimately you were repulsed by doing so. You had believed you were a coward, so you attempted to act in the way you thought cowards should act. But you failed. Hence, you are not a coward. All very subconscious, very Jungian, completely normal. Do I sound like a psychiatrist? I'm so sorry."

"What we mean, Kevin," Miss Betty said, "and I think I have this correct, is that the bird business stems from your mixed-up feelings. Isn't that it, Agatha?"

"Yes, Betty, that's it," Miss Agatha said. "That's it. Anger and guilt are powerful emotions, not to be trifled with." She cocked her head, slightly. "And of course, there is more, I think. Another layer Kevin, am I right?"

"I don't know," he said, and he was conscious that he squinted his eyes as he tried to clear his head.

"Yes, there is," she said. "Another layer. One that affects us all. It's as old as me—older, I'm afraid."

"What's that?" Kevin said.

"I think it's because he was a black fellow."

He wasn't sure that he heard her right. "What?" And all he had in him, all that had come before and went away with his father, had not made it any clearer.

"I said, if there's another level here, maybe it's something you need to admit to yourself. The other man was a Negro. Does that make you angry?"

"You mean, angrier than if he'd been white?"

"Of course, dear," Miss Betty chimed in, cheerily. "What else is there?"

"But why would it matter to me who killed him? He's dead, isn't that enough? How much angrier can you get?"

"You'd be surprised," Miss Agatha said. "And it does matter. To some, anyway. We knew your father. A dear man, and your mother, too. A lovely couple. I know what they thought about these issues. But they are adults, as are Betty and I. We've had time, years, to think about it, to live it. But you've had two months to think about it, at least in the way you're forced to think about it right now. And I know this neighborhood. I know what people whisper, even do, about things like this."

"And it's not at all pleasant, is it Agatha?" Miss Betty said.

"Not at all," Miss Agatha said. "Not in the least. What we're trying to tell you, Kevin, is very simple, at least inasmuch as this bird business goes." Her voiced trailed off a bit, and he leaned forward to listen, rattling his teacup.

"Don't," she said, then leaned in to whisper, "let the neighborhood . . . tell you what to think."

"And do!" Miss Betty shouted. They both jumped back in their seats.

"Betty!" Miss Agatha. "You mustn't shout like that."

"Oh!" Miss Betty said. "I'm so sorry. Kevin, did I startle you?"

"No, not really," he said. It was, whatever it was, happening fast.

"Well, I am sorry," she said, "but aren't I right Agatha? I mean, I think it's 'think and do,' isn't it?"

"Yes, dear," Miss Agatha said. "It's think and do. You're entirely correct and I think young Kevin has got that part, don't you, Kevin?"

Miss Agatha reached across the table and placed her hand over his. It was cool and smooth, dry like a newspaper. She cleared her throat. "Kevin," she said. "You are well loved. And no obligation is more sacred than accepting that love with every ounce of your being. I know this as I know my life. For heaven's sake, dear. Don't fuck it up." She leaned back, withdrawing her hand slowly. She glanced at Miss Betty and smiled.

"Well, that's that!" Miss Betty said, clapping her hands once again. "Hasn't this been fun? Kevin, you haven't touched your tea. Shall I warm it up for you?"

"No," he said, thunderstruck. "No, thank you."

"Betty," Miss Agatha said. "I believe it's time for the note."

"The note, of course. It wouldn't do to forget the note." Miss Betty pushed back from the table and walked out of the room, calling, "You just wait right there. I think I remember where I put it." Her voice trailed off.

Miss Agatha chuckled. "She's a bit of a pip, isn't she?"

He nodded. He knew if he tried to speak it would come out in squeaks.

She leaned in close again. "It's a note to your mother. You mustn't open it, of course, but don't worry. We have not, and will not, mention the birds."

"Thanks," he croaked.

"I trust all that is behind us anyway, isn't it dear?"

He nodded again. "What's in the note?" he rasped.

"Kevin," she said, and squinted and looked off over his shoulder. "What is it you want to do when you get older? What do you want to be?"

"Alive," he said, without even thinking about it. Not that he could have.

"Well, there is alive and there's alive," she said. "I think truly alive is best."

Miss Betty sauntered back into the room, waving a small envelope. "Look, Agatha! It was on the credenza, right where I left it. Isn't that marvelous?"

"Marvelous, Betty. It's lovely when things work out that way."

Miss Betty handed the note to Kevin. It seemed to be a presentation, offered with both hands and, he would have sworn, a curtsey. It was sealed, about the size of a birthday card, with the words "Mrs. Mary Mahoney" on the front.

"It's just a little business between your mother and the two of us," Miss Agatha said. "Nothing to worry about. Just hand it over to her and be off, easy as pie. Would that be all right, Kevin?"

"Yes," Kevin said He turned it over a few times. It felt like a card, nothing more. He stood, then Miss Agatha stood slowly, and Miss Betty put her hand on his shoulder. Her eyes were wet, but she leaned over and kissed him lightly on the cheek with dry lips. Miss Agatha circled the table and grasped both his hands, then cocked her head and offered a tired smile, and pulled him in to kiss him as well. He noted, through his haze, that she wore the same plummy perfume as her sister.

"Now run along, it's been lovely chatting with you," she said.

"Thanks," he said. Christ. He felt like crap. "Thanks for the tea." He turned and walked out the door, his legs slightly rubbery.

When he reached the bottom of the stoop, Miss Betty sang out, "Come by any time, Kevin."

--

He walked through the front door in a daze, into the foyer, the note heavy in his hand. He knew, he trusted completely, that the sisters would be true to their word and wouldn't have mentioned the birds, or Basil. But it was still a note. His mother called out from the kitchen, "Is that you, Kev?"

"Yes."

"Don't go out again, we're having dinner soon."

He spied a stack of mail on the hallway side table. "What are we having?" he shouted, and pulled the envelope from his back pocket.

"Ravioli with meatballs, your favorite. And salad."

"Great," and he turned the envelope over in his hand again, held it up to the light from the front door window.

Not a clue. He slipped it into the middle of the mail pile. "What's for dessert?"

"A treat," she called out. "Colleen's been asking for cannolis. I have three fresh ones, vanilla, from Levecchi's."

"Can't wait," he shouted, and he realized his face and neck were moist with sweat. "I'll be in my room."

He walked upstairs, stopped at the bathroom to splash water on his face, caught himself in the mirror. "So," he said, "three cannolis."

He went to his bedroom and took the rifle from under the bed and held it for a moment, turning it over as he had the note. It was a beautiful thing, a good weight, and the stock shone in the late afternoon sun. He was still sweating, but, in an instant, calm as he'd ever been.

"And so," he said again. He gauged what it would take, then brought up his leg and brought the rifle down, hard, across his knee. The barrel snapped off, and small wood splinters fell to the floor. "Three it is."

END

DANCING

Back then, Doreen had what she called benefits. They were parties, really, loud, besotted, and edgy affairs.

"I'm hosting a benefit tomorrow night," she'd say to my father. "For the Assumption of our Lord Polio League. Try not to be pathetic."

He would nod his head and later, of course, go with pathetic.

It was at the polio party that I saw Doreen—my mother insisted we call her by her first name; she apparently thought it risqué and intimate and bohemian—with her arms around a man whose back I didn't know. I thought they were dancing. Their room, my father's study, was darkened by moon clouds, and jumpy big band music boomed from the hi-fi in the formal dining room at the other end of the long hallway, where the sounds of hissing spritzers and raw laughter indicated the party was on its usual course.

It would be years before I fully understood what I saw, even though Susan would try in her own way to explain it to me that same night. By the time I did understand, the memory would have become, in retrospect, prescient: My father would have drifted away from our family several times, and finally for good, humiliated by his oblique and tedious dispute with alcohol, with Doreen, with his life. And Doreen would have taken a third cynical trip down the altar, she, too, the bad judge.

But the night I saw the two in the study I didn't fully understand her hair dripping over the man's shoulders, or their soft whispers and quick breaths. Still, I sensed drama. The scene had the quality of an opera, like the one my father once took us to see in Atlanta: seen but not understood, language and movement foreign and florid.

I jerked away, unnerved, from the slit in the doorway and resumed my furtive trip through the back doors and hallways of our rambling Southern Federal–style house, a house that had passed through three generations of my mother's ancient and wealthy family, a house so massive it had crushed them all.

I returned upstairs, breathless, having dodged my swaying father as he exited the kitchen. I had been half holding my breath since I'd seen Doreen in the study, and was anxious to get back upstairs before my father came up to check on Susan and Billy and me, and the two Beazley boys. His visits would become infrequent as the night progressed. Finally there would be none.

I stumbled into the room, flopped down on a bed, and sucked air. In the faint moonlight I could see their faces, wide at the nostrils and eyes. They sensed a story. John Beazley broke the silence.

"Well, Dub, what did you see?"

"Nothing," I said. I wished I hadn't. Seen it, I mean.

"Chicken, you didn't even go down," Billy said. He rolled his eyes and sang in a whisper, "Chicken, chicken."

"What about the rum punch? You were supposed to see how far down the punch was." This was from Joe Beazley.

"Same as before, no change," I said. "And you, Billy, I was down there longer than you, than anybody. You want me to bop your nose, you just say that again."

My little brother smiled. "What else?" he whispered.

I blathered on. I said something about the music and about loud conversations and small dough-wrapped sausages. I told them about Mrs. Clarendon, whom I had seen lurching toward the bathroom, covering her mouth while making the sound of a wounded deer.

They all gasped. "Who?"

"Missus Clarendon. The teacher."

They sighed, relieved it wasn't one of our parents. Susan laughed loudest. "Well, that's a hoot. Missus Clarendon. Missus *Ralph* Clarendon. That's great." She looked at me, fierce and straight. "Dub," she said, "I get to tell this at school. I claim it."

Protesting always proved useless with Susan, who was stronger and always seemed closer to the truth than anyone else I knew. Yet, reflexes are also strong, and I objected: "No way."

"I'm the oldest here, Dub. What I say goes as far as the moon. Besides, you wouldn't tell it right anyway. You lose the story." She glared at the Beazley boys and Billy. "That goes for all of you."

"Then I won't tell you what I really saw." I regretted this as soon as I said it.

"What did you *really* see," Joe Beazley said, "a naked lady?"

Billy, youngest of us all, said, "Yeah, a naked lady?"

"Shush, Billy," my sister hissed. "What was it, Dub?"

"I'll just keep it to myself. It wasn't anything."

Susan's brow furrowed and she stroked her hair for a moment; in the years to come I would see that stroke often, a flip of the bangs between her scissors fingers. I would see it as she observed my father slowly giving up. I would see it as my mother brought new and strange men into the house, some who leered at Susan as if she were fruit. It was to become her signal of imminent danger.

"Tell me, Dub," she said. She squinted, tilted her head slightly. "Alone if you'd like."

"It isn't worth it," I said.

"Dub, tell me."

"Okay, I saw Doreen dancing."

Susan was startled. Joe Beazley said, "They never dance at these parties."

"Yeah, you're wrong," Billy said.

Susan exhaled. "Go on, Dub." The moon was bright across her face, and her forehead tightened. "Go on," she said.

"They were dancing," I said, "that's all."

"What did you see, exactly?" she said.

"She was dancing with this man. I don't know him."

"Where?" she said.

"In Dad's room. In the study." I felt nauseated, as I did on a roller coaster.

The Beazley boys and Billy were silent.

"What makes you think they were dancing?" she said.

I answered from the core of my experience. "Because they were moving slow, like they do in the movies."

"Who else was dancing?"

"Nobody."

"Nobody?" and she shut her eyes.

"They were alone in the room. They were alone, I think." I almost couldn't remember.

A gauzy silence wrapped its way around us, and Susan stood up in a quick movement. "I'm going down," she said.

Joe Beazley opened his mouth to protest. He thought it might have been his turn.

"Joe, I can and I will do something very dangerous to you if you say one word. You know I will." Susan walked to the door, cracked it open, and cocked her ear to the hall. "Don't any of you move an inch." She walked out and shut the door, silently.

And we waited, confused by Susan's reaction. Years later I would remember a clock ticking loudly somewhere in the bedroom, ticking for me, signaling directly to me that my betrayal was a unique one. I alone had caused Susan to move quickly and ominously.

The boys kept to their private thoughts. The Beazleys downed imaginary airplanes with their fingers, and Billy crawled up on the bed and dangled his legs from the side, humming a child's song. We waited. We waited twenty minutes.

She walked upright, back into the bedroom.

Susan dropped to her knees and held her finger to her lips, shushing us. We all moved close and waited for her to start. She glanced at each of us in turn, and when she came to me her eyes glistened like oiled marbles. She lingered, then turned to the other boys.

"Well," she whispered, and began slowly, hushed.

Susan told us who was drinking what, that the women were gossiping in the kitchen about Miss Bobby LeAnn Tremont's short skirts (they all think she's too chubby for that type of attire), and that Mr. Beazley was delivering his old lecture about thieving lawyers, because he himself is a goddamn lawyer goddammit, and if he had the money he'd buy himself a State Supreme Court appointment like the rest of them. The Beazley boys, his sons, flushed at Susan's use of their father's word, but were silenced by her tight urgency.

She paused and took a breath. "And Mister Greerson's cigarette has burned clear down to his fingers, but he's still standing there talking and not noticing that he's near on fire. He must be drunker than a worm in an apple, or maybe he's got leprosy or something," she giggled. "You know they can't feel things." I wasn't precisely sure, but the word itself brought a horror.

"And then," she said, "Miss Lucy Tiggles, that's the mayor's secretary, was out on the back verandah with the other ladies, talking about her boyfriend. I'm getting the impression a lot of ladies talk about their boyfriends. Her back was turned to me so I couldn't hear the whole story, but what she does is she picks up her hands and holds them about a foot apart, like she was describing a fish she caught, but all those ladies laughed so hard I'm sure it wasn't that kind of fish she was talking about." Susan snorted. We were silent, and a hot flush crossed my face.

"What kind of a fish was it?" John Beazley said. His brother and Billy exchanged frowns.

Susan cleared her throat. "Well, it doesn't matter anyhow." She sighed.

"Now listen," she said. "We have got to be quiet and we have to get to bed right now."

I'd begun to think it might be safe, that there was reprieve from the dancing business, when Joe Beazley opened his mouth, "But Susan, what about your—"

"Shush up, Joe Beazley, I haven't got time to talk. None of us do. Get to bed." She shot him a steady glance, and he backed down. "You jump into bed with your brother. Billy, you get to sleep by yourself tonight. I'm going to sleep with Dub in the big bed." She glanced at me.

Billy snorted a giggle, clearly pleased. Susan handed him a stuffed lion with button eyes. She said, "Now be quiet and go to sleep, all of you."

They lingered for a moment, but sensed her power. Within a few minutes they had slipped into their beds, Billy humming again to himself. Susan walked to the door and cracked it open to listen to the party below. I slipped into the sheets, she closed the door silently, and came to bed.

My sister's skin, freckled and nearly translucent, caught the moonlight and moved with it as she crossed the room. Her ankles, neck, and wrists were long, her eyes bright green. Pictures of my mother at Susan's age showed the same frail limbs and features, and I was uncomfortable as I assessed their beauty. They were both striking, their mouths severe. When they were children, they both looked like women.

When she reached the bed she knelt on the covers facing me and leaned. Her long ginger hair fell and brushed my lips lightly. Susan's eyes were still wet marbles, from her storytelling and laughing, I thought. She sighed through her nose and brought her hand to my forehead. She seemed sad and lovely, like the last scene of a movie. She cocked her head sideways, then moved to her side of the bed.

As she crawled in she said, "Hi."

My head was light. It was her smells, the baby powders, shampoo, cold toe smells. Her flannel gown was fresh and laundered. I looked at the ceiling and said, "So what happened?"

She propped herself on one elbow. "We used to sleep together before Billy was born, remember?"

It had been only a few years since we'd stopped sharing the same bed. It seemed distant.

She shifted. "It's sort of nice, isn't it?"

It was. My body was tense and I felt I needed to stretch my muscles, uncoil myself. She rolled over and my head lifted on a waft of her. Her smells were like limbs of her body, stretching and reaching. I looked at her and I knew this: I wanted to dance with her.

"Dub, you're breathing hard. Where's your pump?"

"It's not the asthma. I'll be okay."

A cloud moved in front of the moon and I lost her face. She said, "So what is it?"

I rolled over on my stomach. "Just out of breath, is all."

"Oh," she said, and socked me lightly in the small of the back. She left her hand there.

"Did you see Doreen?" I said.

Susan drew back her hand. "Yeah, Doreen," she said, and flopped back on the pillow. "I saw them."

"Dancing?"

Susan stared at the ceiling. She pumped her arms up and down, push-ups against the air. She studied her nails. Then she stroked her hair. I sat upright. "Well?"

"She's a madwoman," she said, and she whimpered, a whispered wail, a desperate sound.

I reached over and put my hand on her shoulder. Her back was soft, and damp.

She said, "Remember the time Doreen went crazy when someone stole her fifty dollars?"

"Sure," I said. It was early summer in the year before Billy was born. It had happened like this: At dinner one night, without any indication she'd been angry, Doreen had slapped her dinner fork onto the table, next to her wine.

"Well, well," she'd said.

Dad blinked. "What's that, Doreen?" He looked like a dog that's just seen a bunch of boys walking toward it with tin cans.

"Oh, just the money."

"What money?"

"My money, of course," she said, and smiled at him. "Who else has money?"

"What about your money?" Dad said. He emphasized the word "your."

"It's gone, isn't it. And I think someone took it. Susan Louise? Dub?"

"Not me," we both said, in unison.

"Well, then. The Good Fairy took it."

"Doreen," Dad said. He buttered some bread. "Where did you put the money, and how much was it?"

She looked past his shoulder. Her eyes were small slits in her head. "A fifty dollar bill, on the counter," she said.

"Maybe it blew behind the stove," Dad said.

"Fifty dollar bills don't blow away," she said, evenly.

"Or do they?" She turned slowly to me. "Dub, empty your pockets."

"I hardly think that's necessary," Dad said.

"I do think I know what I'm doing, Mister Jurisprudence," she said. "I do think I do."

"Doreen, please," Dad said.

"I didn't take it," I said, truthfully. But it sounded weak. I knew my right eye twitched. Susan sat rigid in her seat, her eyes widening.

"I said empty your pockets."

"Dub, why don't you and Susan excuse yourselves," Dad said.

Doreen turned to him. "No!" she growled. "You two stay right here at this table. Dub, empty."

It was at times like this when I saw an unnatural fire in Doreen's eyes. It was a reckoning time; the Atlanta Symphony could be playing the 1812 Overture overhead and she wouldn't blink an eye at the cannons. I stood up and tossed a penknife, two stones, fifty-eight cents, and a rubber on the table. It was a Trojan. Unopened, of course.

Doreen's eyes widened. "Jesus Mary and Joseph," she whispered.

I stood at attention, sort of.

"Dub," Dad said, "what in hell is that?"

"May I be excused?" Susan said. This was apparently going to be too much for her loyalty to handle.

"Sit, Susan!" Doreen said. "Do you know what that *is*, Dub?"

"I think, maybe, it's a rubber. Isn't it?"

Doreen gasped. "Good God, don't you ever use that word in this house!"

"Dub," Dad said, "where did you get that?"

"I just found it. I was riding my bike down by the pond."

"Get that, that *thing* off my kitchen table," Doreen hissed, and slammed down her wine glass. Red liquid splashed over her fist. I picked up the foil-wrapped condom.

"Don't touch it!" she shouted. "What are you *doing*?"

"Getting it off the table?"

"Drop it!" she said.

"But, Doreen—"

"What were you *doing* with it?"

"Just carrying it around," I said. That was the truth.

"Walter!" she said, and glared at Dad. "Deal with this."

He stared at the Trojan as if it were a mystery, and maybe it was, in its own way. Then he stood and leaned over the table to pick it up.

"Walter! Don't touch it!"

"It's not radioactive, for Pete's sake."

"But, it's, it's *a thing*!"

Dad picked a fork up from the table. "For Christ's sake, Doreen," he said, and stabbed the condom with the fork. "It's not like it's been opened."

"Sweet Jesus, I should hope not!"

Dad wrapped the foil Trojan in a napkin and threw it in the trash.

"The fork," Doreen said. "The fork, the fork, *the fork*!" Dad tossed the fork into the rubbish.

"May I be excused?" Susan said.

"What in God's name were you doing with it?" Doreen screeched.

"I just found it," I said.

"But you *know* what it's for," she said, and poured more wine with shaking hands.

I did, in a vague and rudimentary sort of way. At first I thought it was an odd pack of chewing gum, but when I saw the word "Trojan," I knew that I'd found it, the Holy Grail. I'd heard the boys at school talking about them, and was thrilled at having one in the flesh, so to speak. Of course, at the time, using it, or even opening it, was incomprehensible.

"No, I don't know what it's for," I said.

"Dub," Dad said, "maybe we better have a talk."

"Talk?" Doreen said. "Aren't we good little fathers and sons. No, what this needs is discipline." She stood up and leaned over the table.

"I'd like to be excused," Susan said.

"Go!" Doreen said. And Susan left the table like a Japanese geisha, quietly and with purpose.

"Doreen, it's just a kid thing," Dad said. "He was curious, and now he knows what it is. He didn't mean any harm."

"Oh really? You knew exactly what it was, didn't you, Dub. Don't lie."

I glanced at Dad, and looked away, quickly. "No, ma'am."

Doreen glared for a moment, then her faced screwed tight and she reached out and slapped me hard across the face. "Liar!" she screamed. "Liar, liar!" She made a fist and whacked my shoulder. Dad jumped up from his seat and grabbed her arm.

"Leave him alone!" he said. "It's over. And Dub doesn't have the money. Neither does Susan. It's lost!"

"I know that, goddammit!" she said.

Dad's eyes narrowed. "Dub, go outside with your sister."

"Yes, sir," I said, and bolted out to find Susan sitting up in the big weeping willow tree in the backyard. I climbed up, my face still hot from the slap. Susan gazed out over the house as a cool night breeze picked up.

"You just had to toss it out on the table," she said.

"She would've just gone through my pockets and found I was trying to hold back."

"And you knew what it was?" From the house, the muffled sounds of the argument surged and subsided: shouts, thumps, and finally, the sobbing. Sometimes he sobbed, sometimes she sobbed.

"Sort of."

"It's revolting."

"I know."

"What possessed you to pick it up?"

I shrugged my shoulders and listened to the house, now quiet.

"You know," she said, "in her mind you've already gone to hell. We've all gone to hell."

"Whatever."

"Lord," she said.

—–—

Susan lay on her back on the bed, staring at the ceiling. "I never told you what really happened about the money," she said.

I was confused. The incident was ancient and had been resolved, or so I thought. "You found it and gave it to her, didn't you?" I remembered the next night, when things were calm again. The dinner table had been silent, as if it were empty.

"I gave it to her," Susan said. "But I didn't find it. I took it from my allowance savings."

"Why?"

"Because at first I thought you took it and you were so scared of her you'd never give it back. Or admit to it."

I protested. I hadn't taken it.

"I know, Dub. I know that now. But I didn't when I gave it to her the next day."

"So, how do you know now?"

Susan swallowed. "When I gave her the money she was all puffy and feeling bad, you know how she gets, and she said, she said to me, I know you didn't find it behind the stove, Susan Louise. I told her yes I did but she just took it and said I checked behind the stove and I also know it's not in your character to steal money and besides, I know what happened. Then she said I'll hold on to it for now until I resolve this, now scoot and leave me alone. And I scooted."

I felt left out, and said so.

"Well," she continued, and her voice cracked. Her toes, warm now, brushed against my leg in an agitated motion. Her oily eyes were shiny with the moon. "About a week after that, Daddy took me for a ride to get some ice cream. In the car he handed me a new fifty dollar bill and he said take it Susie because I know you used your own money in that thing. And I said no I didn't but he said just take it and let's keep it between us, sweetie. He said that he knew I didn't steal it and you didn't steal it, and he put the money in my hand and said I was a good girl and then he said now shush, honey, you know I love you more than anything in the whole world, you kept your mother happy and that's always a good thing to do because you know how she takes things real hard."

Susan turned over and closed her eyes before her face hit the pillow. I could hear only her breathing. I felt heavy, fat with her story, sluggish and stupid.

"Susan," I whispered, "what about the study? Did you see them?"

"Yes, of course. They were just dancing. Like you said."

I reached over and touched her shoulder. Her back rose up and down, rapidly, as it would for most of the night.

END

AT TIMES LIKE THIS

The director listened for a moment before he said, in an even tone, "Yes, yes I understand." He held the phone away from his ear and squinted, as if the person on the other end was speaking loudly, or upbraiding him. Which, as it turned out, was hardly the case. "Yes, as soon as we can. Sure, I'll call tomorrow. Same time." His voice faltered at the end of the sentence, went soft.

He pulled the phone away again and turned it toward him, examining the earpiece. "Wright's mother is dead," he said to the phone, and turned to Lenny. Blinked.

"Oh my God," Miriam said, across the room. Her eyes had gone wide.

"Jesus," Lenny whispered. At that moment, at the moment Miriam said it, he pictured Wright's face, bright somehow, with screwed-in eyebrows, Wright telling him that his mother was desperately ill. That was how Wright had said it, she was "desperately ill." Not that he knew

Wright all that well, at least not well enough to expect the guy to say something like that to him. It's just that out there in the bush, in the middle of no one and nothing familiar to you, a person will blurt out truths that are close to him and leave them there, hanging like that. It was as if the act of airing your fears would cause them to wither against themselves. Like confession.

Wright had said something about it, about how four months before he was due to leave for his two-year Peace Corps stint in Botswana his mother had learned she'd had cancer. He'd said he was worried his mother would die while he was out here in the godforsaken bush. Again, a phrase, the "godforsaken bush." He'd said it to a group that included some Brits and Americans, all expats, Lenny was in the group, and it was after several more than a couple of beers at the President Hotel in Gaborone. Wright saying how he wondered if he'd done the right thing, and it had come out in that animated, bright-eyed way of his. Looking for sanction. It was disconcerting. When he'd said it, the Brits and the Americans cleared their throats and glanced down, embarrassed for the guy but somehow hating him, too, that was evident. "That's bad bloody luck, mate," Gingers said, but without much conviction.

And now of course, she was dead. Of course he knew what was next.

"Someone's got to tell him," the director said.

"That would be me," Lenny said, already feeling the dread rise.

"Yes. Yes, it would."

Miriam nodded, slowly.

"I mean, someone's got to go up there to tell him,"

the director said, and pointed his thumb in a northward direction. He squinted hard to make his point.

"That would be me," Lenny repeated. "I mean it. I'll do it." Suddenly feeling adamant about it, acting as if he had to prove it.

"It'll take two nights to get it done," the director said. "Overnight up on the train, another day into the bush and back. Find him, pack him up, and get him back here."

"Be back in two days," Lenny said. "Friday."

"We'll have the tickets ready for him when he gets here," the director said. "The plane tickets. Miriam, we can do that, yes?"

"I'll have them," Miriam said in her clipped Brit-Botswana accent. "But," she said. "But why not just call him? I mean, send e-mail or so. Tell him to come down here, post haste."

"It's his mother," the director said. "Besides, no phones at the school. No computers, no e-mail. The nearest fax is probably in Francistown. We can't call the police in Francistown, they'd take three days to even move on it." He looked embarrassed for a moment, glanced at the other two, lingered on Miriam apologetically, having revealed his unprofessional and wholly realistic bias. "Anyway, by the time anyone gets to him, Lenny will have found him and they'd be halfway back here. It's policy, anyway. A warm body tells another warm body in person that his mother's gone cold. It's policy."

"Jo," Miriam said, and exhaled at the director's words.

"I don't mind," Lenny said, perhaps too loudly, and

he didn't mind, at least in theory, right then and there. But this was Africa. Things could change.

"Why didn't the family or Washington tell us some days ago, before she died?" Miriam said. "That would have given him time, maybe even he could have been home before she passed."

"Who knows what they were thinking," the director said. "People are insane at times like this."

"I'd better get going," Lenny said, and he turned to Miriam. "Can you ring me up some train tickets? One going up, two returning. I'll go home and pack something, get my kit together."

He left thinking he'd have to make up something, something formal, some kind of speech to tell the man that his mother was dead, that he'd missed her last moments, her last words, a final embrace, or just the sweet, humid breath of delivery.

An hour later he was at the train station, alone in a second class car on the Botswana Railways overnighter to Francistown. After which he'd catch a half-day's taxi ride out to the village of Tutume and the secondary school there, where he hoped to find Wright. The train sat on the tracks, rumbling like a big cat, and he stared out the window at the low hum of activity.

Small cooking fires oozed the acrid smoke of burning acacia, and vendors, mostly women, carried fragrant pans of roasted chicken and fat cakes on their heads, fist-sized gobs of luscious fried dough, offering them up to the windows. The passengers grabbed lustily, tossing coins and wadded paper bills into the pans. Lenny wasn't hungry. His stomach was already knotted, he was queasy. He had a central problem. What if it was his own mother and some guy he hardly knew traveled two days to tell him the bad news, how would he react? Would he cry outright? Would he turn away, embarrassed to be in front of everyone? Or would he be angry at the bearer of news for having the knowledge, that power over him. It didn't matter. All that was fantasy, none of it true. If he'd heard the news that his mother had suddenly died, it would be no more personal than if he'd heard some obscure movie star had died, though he'd be mildly surprised that the vodka and Vicodin and Vegas hadn't done her in earlier. Then he'd wonder why the hell they'd even wasted the effort to send someone to find him, because it didn't matter, he wouldn't be going home. There was no home. She'd been more or less dead to him anyway for, what, eight years now. Ever since she'd taken up with her newest boyfriend. Or maybe a little before that, when he'd begun to notice the flight in her eyes, how she'd gaze out the kitchen window, both hands wrapped around a tumbler, making an offering to the open road. The way she looked at the walls of the house, the lawn, the furniture, her own kids. Like there was nothing else she'd rather not be looking at. Then she'd found her salvation and delivery in her walking cliché, a Viva Las Vegas savant, twenty years older and dressed in wide-lapelled sports jackets, a mouth-breather whose smell was open and decadent, and who, behind his new girlfriend's back, stared at Lenny's sister like she was a prime Vegas Delmonico.

Then they finally did it—they were compelled to do it because it was in their DNA, in their life scripts—they packed off to the actual Las Vegas to pursue the actual cliché. Married in an Elvis chapel, said they'd be back in five days, but after five weeks and double as many phone calls, Lenny knew it for sure, knew it from the sound in her voice, that she had a new life, the old one was long gone and buried, and she was somewhere else in body, mind and what she had left of spirit. So at twenty-one years old, his sister nineteen, Lenny was on his own.

That was eight years ago, and when he thought about it now he knew that as the train was his witness, when the day came that he heard his mother died, he'd cry like a baby.

The train's fake whistle sounded and Lenny started. He'd been drifting off, mulling over his speech to Wright. He sat up, stretched his legs, and heard the conductor outside his window, a fat, white South African, shout, "'Board!"

Lenny went back to his speech. "Hey, man, sorry, your mom died." Best to start from the base. But the "hey man," part sounded flip when he said it again. Or, "Wright, your mother passed away." Dignified, yet somehow formulaic. He wasn't the kind of person who said "passed away." He tried, "Wright, get your bags packed, bad news at home, sorry, it's your mom. No, I'm not sure what the situation is at this very minute, but your family wants you."

That last one surprised him. The lying. But the words seemed comfortable, which made it feel like the right thing to do. At least while he was looking Wright straight in the face. He could just say it, and let Wright make his own conclusions. How Wright would react was the second part of the equation. Maybe he'd be calm and say, "Sure, I knew it was going to happen, let's go." Or not. Maybe he'd stare for a moment, disbelief overwhelming him, the tears under his eyeballs welling up and bubbling down his cheeks. Maybe he'd sob, drop to his knees, fall face first in the dust. Maybe he'd need a hug.

"Christ, no," Lenny said out loud, startling himself. He knew he wouldn't do the lying. It would have to be straight up and out his mouth, no screwing around. More like, "Wright, I'm sorry, but your mother died."

The train jerked and squealed, and pulled out slowly from the station, and from Gaborone. He was alone in his second class compartment, all red leather and brass, two sets of unmade bunk beds stacked against the walls. The porter would be around later, offering to set up the bedding. Lenny began to smell the vastness of the Kalahari, the clean, cool, nighttime air that slid off the desert through his open window. A hint of jacaranda, a whiff of cooking fires, the mist of cow effluvia in the dust. The train relaxed him, rocking gently, but he was wary about slipping into sleep this early. He could be joined at any stop by another lone traveler ushered into the compartment by the porter. It was a slow time, a weekday night, and there was little chance of the train being crowded, but he didn't want to be asleep if someone was shown the door.

He got up, decided to keep moving. He headed for the bar car, which lay in the middle of the train between second and third class. He'd been it in before, it was always happy-loud and crowded, boisterous, like everyone going on long trips was compelled to drink heavily until they rolled off the train. And so it was. Two dozen small tables lined the sides, and a small throng crowded up against the bar. He joined them, shouted here and there, waved some money, finally got his beer. He walked back to a table and sat, thinking he'd be sitting there again, maybe even the same table, with Wright on the return trip. Better than sitting in the sleeping car, the two of them wondering what to say.

The crowd was overwhelmingly African and mostly men. He was the only white in sight. It meant little to him. In the early days he was aware of the color difference, wondering not if, but to what degree, they resented him. Aware of their eyes on him on the street, on the buses, when the local butcher called him to the front of the throng—there were no queues in Africa—aware that when he politely refused the butcher with a nod and a "Thanks, I'm fine" gesture, the throng would roll their eyes at his liberal largesse. Aware that when he took girls home from the local watering holes it was his color they saw first.

Now, he went with it, easily. After four years, he was fluent enough in Setswana to diffuse most situations, and bridge some of the gaps color had carved out.

Two men and a woman entered noisily from the third class side of the car. The thin double doors slammed open from the center like the swinging doors of an old-time western saloon, and they tumbled in. They were drunk or high or both, and Lenny clutched his beer a little tighter as they glanced around the room, red eyes dancing. They were young, about his own age, and each of the men had a hand on one of the woman's arms. She was on the fleshy side of thin, with a conservative, long dress that buttoned from her throat to mid-calf. She had on a dressy hat, sort of like a bowler with lace and a veil, the type Lenny saw on the church matrons on Sunday. Not the best getup for this climate, and not the type of outfit you saw on a drunk in a train bar car. He was intrigued, glanced sideways, wondering what the story was. The girl glanced over at him, unsteady, and as the men led her to the bar by her elbows she smiled and turned her head back, and over her shoulder did the movie star thing, the wink. He didn't respond. He watched them buy their beers, and soon they turned back to the bar car, looking for a spot to sit.

Lenny had three chairs open at his table, thinking it had to have come to this. This is still the movie playing itself out, a high drama script where they all sit down with him to make small talk while the girl, drunk and oblivious to her male companions' smoldering hate for the white man, makes jokes and flirts dangerously with the stranger. Eventually going too far, touching him or something. Then the shouts, the recriminations, the finger pointing, the chairs pushed back and toppled over. The knives.

Instead, the two let go of the girl to stop at a table full of men, laughing and shaking hands all around. She made a straight shot for Lenny, for the table, and sat down, exhaling loudly. Her eyes were looping rapidly, nearly vibrating.

"You look like a Peace Corps," she said. She hadn't completely focused on his face yet.

"You look like schoolteacher," he said. She laughed, and tipped her beer to her lips, squinting through the bottle as if she were sighting him over the barrel of a rifle.

"I am a schoolteacher," she said.

"You're not acting like a schoolteacher," he said. "At least, not the ones I know."

"Oh, and how am I supposed to be acting?" Still smiling. "Like a good girl, like one of my students? A woman can drink as well, you know? I am a modern woman. What is the harm in it?"

"None," Lenny said. "None at all. It's fine by me. *O mang?*"

"Thandi," she said. "So you speak the language. And yours?"

"Lenny. Leonard."

"I like that you speak our language," she said. "You honor us."

"No," Lenny said, sliding into the game. "It is you who honor me."

"*O tswa kae*?" she said, her eyes now moist and twinkling.

"America," he said. "Las Vegas, I guess. *Le wena*?"

"I'm from Ramotswa," she said, slurring it. "A little village up north. That's where I am now going. I am going home."

He thought he caught a slight sigh, a wistful exhale.

"I know the place," he said. "And your two friends. They are, what, students of yours?"

He'd caught her sipping the beer and she choked, laughing. "What? Do they look like schoolchildren? Jo. These are my brothers, that's all."

"You're traveling to Ramotswa together?"

"Yes, yes. Well, no, not really, they are dropping me there. Like that. I am going to my family."

The two African men glanced over, looking for her, frowns building on their faces.

She saw Lenny glance up, then turned toward them as the two men made their way across the car.

She turned back quickly, undid the third button on her dress, and reached inside her bra. She came out with a palm-size change purse, beaded, blue and glittery, and placed it on the table. Her eyes looped again. "I've had too much," she said.

She twisted in her chair, and looked for the two men, raised her forefinger to them, the universal gesture for "give me a minute." It stopped them, and they glanced at each other, confused.

She turned back, smirking. "They can wait, isn't it."

"Guess they can."

"So, you, Leonard, where are you off to tonight?"

"Francistown," he said. "Long story."

"Tell it," she said, and her eyes invited him to go on for a long time.

Then the men reached her shoulders, one on each side, still the grim looks. The one on the right said in Setswana, "Let's go." Staring at Lenny.

"I'll be coming soon," she said. Her gaze also on Lenny.

"Now. *Jaanong*," the man said, calmly, but emphasizing it.

"No. *Not* exactly *now*," she said in English. She said to Lenny: "My mother has died, isn't it. That is why I am going back home."

The guy placed his hand on her forearm, she paid no attention. The skirt button was still undone, and it stretched out to reveal the pink lace of her bra. She slid the change purse across the table, and whispered with another wink, "Hold this, I'll be right back."

"What?" Lenny said.

"I said hold this, I'll be—"

"No, I mean, your mother died?"

"Yes. Suddenly. She was not yet fifty." Her face began to turn into itself, and she breathed through her nose, holding back, then unable to hold back, the tears.

"*A re tsamaya*," the man said again. Let's go.

"Shut up," she snapped, and dragged her arm across her face.

The other man took the forearm on his side and they

both pulled her up out of the chair, halfway between gentle and rough.

"Wait for me," she said.

"Are you okay?" Lenny said, dumbstruck.

"Yes, of course. No problems," she sniffed.

"Do you want to go? With them?"

She laughed now. "I'll be right back," she said again.

"Wait!"

"Yes?" she said, even as the two men pulled at her.

"How did you find out?" he said. "Who told you?"

Her brow furrowed and she stared, perplexed, as if language had failed them both at that moment.

"I mean, that your mother died?"

She shrugged her shoulders and the three walked out, the two men guiding her, all rocking with the rhythm of the train, the drunk walk, through the door, back into third class.

Lenny reached over for the change purse. So much in Africa—he knew it then better than he'd known anything in his entire life—so much of Africa was completely out of his grasp, it wouldn't matter if he lived there for thirty years. He just wasn't ever going to get it.

But he did know she wasn't coming back. He would never see her again, never be sure how it worked out for her, at her mother's funeral and all, and after it. Or, now.

He popped open the purse. It contained a one and a five pula note, and loose change. Nothing more. No ID, no papers, no keys. The money was nothing. The purse itself was worth more. He snapped it shut and thought, one more beer, then I'm gone.

The beer went down fast. He thought better of running off like that, and made the decision to wait another twenty minutes. It was a long twenty minutes, lots of watch-checking involved. He was completely aware that the tables were glancing his way, pulling up short if he turned toward them. But he'd made the promise to himself to wait, and twenty minutes seemed reasonable. More than reasonable, given the circumstances.

In what seemed like an instant, like swallows in flight turning on a dime, the drinking crowd thinned out, returning loudly to their compartments and benches for the overnight portion of the trip. He checked his watch again and got up, handed the purse to the bartender, who took it slowly as if he was used to being handed women's purses on a constant basis. Lenny said, "If she comes back, give it to her. There's six pula in it." The bartender nodded. Lenny put a couple of pula notes into his hand, and walked out.

His compartment remained empty, and he found a freshly made bed for him on the bench. He leaned over, filled his hands with a gathering of sheets and breathed in deeply. They were starchy and crisp, and clean. Without undressing, he crawled under the sheet and put his head on the pillow, listening. Once or twice he began to drift off and heard light footsteps in the hallway, and some whispering, which he couldn't make out.

It was an intimate gesture, handing him the purse like that. The promise to return, the order to wait for her, the wink. The wink.

He drifted but never slept, aware that the beers and the gentle rocking of the train and the cool night air should have put him to sleep instantly. But he rocked, and dreamed half-awake.

"Thandi," he said, "I'm sorry, but your mother died. Time to pack up. Come to my compartment."

"I know," she said. "My brothers have told me. Keep the purse, in her memory."

"They aren't your brothers."

"I know," she said.

"I gave the purse to the bartender."

"I know," she said.

Maybe he did sleep, he wasn't completely sure, but suddenly the conductor was in the corridor, rapping on doors with his key, knowing which passengers were disembarking and which doors they were behind. "Francistown," he said in a singsong way, "Francistown!"

The train was slowing down, chugging slightly. Lenny knew he had about thirty minutes before it pulled into the station. He had a headache, and his mouth was dry. It was four-thirty in the morning. He ran the water in the small sink in his compartment and splashed his face, dried it with his sleeve. He grabbed his bag and put it on his lap. The porter came by, knocked, and said, "Tea, sir?"

"Yes, thanks," Lenny said.

The porter opened the door and handed him a mug of rooibos bush tea off a cart, the best tea in the world, sweet, milky and scalding. Lenny paid him, and he was alone again.

An hour later he was in a beat-up, smoking Russian Lada on his way to Tutume. The taxi driver Lenny had hailed, Basiame was his name, was initially confused, then elated. He'd never once in his life gotten an eighty pula round-trip fare, but then this was a white man, whose funds were unlimited and whose mission was undeniably important. They'd never even bothered to haggle. Lenny stated his needs, in Setswana, and Basiame made up a fare on the spot. He was to wait for

Lenny at the secondary school while he fetched someone, presumably another white man, to bring back to
Francistown for the return train trip to Gaborone. He
couldn't believe his luck, and he berated himself for not
asking for more. Still. As he found the westbound road
out of Francistown, he was thinking of a way to hide the
money from his large and overbearing wife.

They didn't speak much. The cattle, the rains, the
villages they passed, this and that. The taxi rumbled and
spewed along the tarmac, a decent road for this part of
the country. "Wright," Lenny said to himself, "Wright,
I'm sorry but your mother died."

And he was sorry. Wright was off-kilter, a bit of an
enigma, but a guy's mother was a guy's mother. His
heart began to pick up pace as they neared the turnoff
to Tutume. It would be twenty minutes of rough road
before they reached the school.

They pulled in to the schoolyard, four or five nondescript, cinderblock buildings in the African veldt. Basiame announced it: "We are here!" The enthusiasm, all
the better for the tip. They both got out of the car.

The nearest building was what served as the adminis-
trative headquarters. Lenny imagined it had a staff room
with an old-fashioned mimeograph machine, a broken
photocopier, and boxes of chalk, paper, and rulers. There
would be a small gas stove to make tea. Chairs and tables.
The lone door opened to the outside, and presumably
another inside door led to the headmaster's office.

The staff room door swung open, and a white man
stepped into the late morning light. Wright. He was
dressed in khaki trousers and sandals, a shortsleeved
shirt with a lion's head print motif, and he carried a canvas duffel bag. He'd had a beard until recently. Or, he

163

still had a beard, half of one. He'd shaved the left half of his face, and half a beard and mustache remained on the right. On top, he'd shaved the right side of his head, and left hair on the left. It was as if he'd drawn a line vertically down his face, bisecting his forehead, nose, and lips. Picasso in the Cubism period.

"Jo," Basiame said, whispered, really. His eyes were wide. "Is this who we are picking up?"

"'Fraid so," Lenny said.

An African man, older, about fifty, stepped out behind Wright. The headmaster. He stepped up to Wright and put his hand on his shoulder. Wright's eyes were red-rimmed, and his lips trembled slightly.

"Dumela," the headmaster said, then dispensed with the usual greetings. "You are here for Mister Wright?"

"I am," Lenny said.

"Well and good."

"Wright," Lenny said, and took a deep breath. His heart hammered. "I'm sorry, but your mother died."

"Understood," Wright said quickly. "She was desperately ill."

"That's right," Lenny said, and held back for a moment. "You knew?"

"Yes, I knew," he said.

"Mister Wright knew it,' the headmaster said. "He knew. You must help him."

"I can see that," Lenny said. He turned back to Wright, blinking. At the hair. "Well. I've got this taxi, we can be in Francistown and on the train by evening. You're going home."

"Understood," Wright said. "I'm packed. Good to go."

"You're ready?"

"She was dreadfully ill," he said.

"Let me take the bag," Lenny said. Basiame, his wide eyes riveted to Wright's head, stepped forward and took the canvas duffel from his hand.

"You okay?" Lenny said.

"Perfect," Wright said, looking at the ground. "Perfecta-monto."

"Wright," Lenny said. "Don't mind me asking, but what's with the look? The hair?"

"Ritual cutting," Wright said. His half-beard quivered with his lips. He was going to cry, Lenny sensed it. "In her memory," Wright said. Then he cried.

Awkward moment. Basiame glanced at Lenny. A white man is supposed to hug another white man, isn't it? African men do not hug white men. Or other African men, for that matter. He waited for Lenny to step forward.

Lenny was thinking: There's never a woman around when you need one. The hugging business was not going to happen. Then the headmaster's hand on Wright's shoulder must have given a squeeze, a nearly imperceptible grip, which had the effect of being enough. Wright caught hold of himself.

"You're going to get on the plane like that?" Lenny said.

"Sure," Wright sobbed. "It's the least I can do."

"They might not let you," Lenny said. "I mean, get on the plane and all. With the hair. Like that."

"Take him, please," the headmaster said, a little too quickly. "He needs help. It will all get sorted out."

Lenny leaned forward, took Wright's arm. "Sure. Let's go. You okay? Let's get in the car."

Wright's head was bowed, his shoulders curved

forward, like he was walking away from the last round of a prizefight. He slid into the back seat of the Lada.

"Thank you," the headmaster said, and practically blessed himself. "Thank you."

"We'll be in touch," Lenny said, and got into the front seat.

They drove the first fifteen minutes in silence, Lenny glancing back at Wright, who stared out the window as if seeing the African veldt for the first time. Idly twirling his half-beard with dirty fingers. Basiame's eyes moved between the road ahead and the rearview mirror, checking on Wright, wondering how he could squeeze more money out of the situation. He decided he would take Lenny aside at one point and ask for hazardous duty pay.

"Because I am transporting a madman," he would say.

"He's not mad, just grieving," Lenny would say.

"He is mad. A complete lunatic. His hair and beard, isn't it, makes him a madman."

"It makes him look like a madman, doesn't make him a madman. Anyway, he's a harmless madman," Lenny would say.

"But he obviously has a razor," Basiame would say. "He may leap from the back seat at any moment and slit my throat. Twenty-five pula extra, it's a bargain."

"Bargain my ass," Lenny would say, because that's how white men talked.

Lenny turned around in his seat. Wright was still staring out the window. "Wright," he said. "I am sorry it had to happen like this."

"Thanks," Wright said.

"You want to talk about it?"

"No," he said to the window, and breathed out heavily. "Not much to say at this point."

"Look, I've got to ask something, though. How did you know?"

"What?"

"I mean, you were packed and ready when we got there. How did you know?"

"You mean that she died?"

"Yes, that your mother—" He paused, thought about it, went for it, "passed away."

Wright turned away from the window and looked straight at Lenny for the first time that day.

"It's something you just know," he said. "She was hideously ill."

Basiame glanced sideways at Lenny, alarm in his eyes. "This will be twenty-five pula extra," he said.

"What?" Lenny said.

"Twenty-five pula," Basiame said.

"What for?" Lenny said.

"You just know," Wright said again. "Two days ago I guess. Got up in the morning, got dressed, got some water from the rain tank. I'd forgotten to fill my twenty-liter at the borehole this week, so I was tapping my rain water. I was brushing my teeth outside the hut, and I felt something behind me. Like when I was a little kid, how she used to stand behind me, making sure I did a good job."

"I meant thirty pula," Basiame whispered. "In advance."

"She used to say, 'That's good, Erin, you're going to have beautiful teeth all your life,'" Wright said.

167

"Your name is Aaron?" Lenny said.

Wright nodded. "Spelled E-R-I-N."

"So you heard her say something. I mean, she was there with you?"

"No, I was just brushing my teeth and all of a sudden I knew my mother died. That's it. Who knows, I don't even know why I'm telling you this."

"You're telling me because I asked, I guess. And it's a memory you have, a good one, and you knew she was sick. Not everyone has those memories." Lenny was aware that he could pile it on, be bitter about, milk it for reasons he didn't understand. But he couldn't. He was already tired of thinking about it.

"She was a good mom," Wright said.

"Moms are good," Lenny said. "The best ones stay that way. It's okay, look, you were ready when we got there. Of course you knew."

"Nothing more to say about it," Wright said. "I was ready and I'm still ready."

"Shaved and ready," Basiame said. His shoulders heaved up as he chuckled to himself.

Wright snickered into the window, leaned forward and tapped Basiame on the shoulder, spoke perfect Setswana. Flawless, Lenny would later say. "Half-shaved, and ready. You see, my friend, I shaved to honor my mother, but she would have been seriously alarmed if she'd ever seen me this way. Would have killed her."

"So I suppose it's a good thing she—" Basiame said, and turned in to the two white men. "No, I didn't say that!"

But he was the first to laugh, hooting and snorting, joined by Wright, who in a minute was sprawled across the back seat holding his sides. Lenny in the front gagged and hollered, glimpsed his mother in the dust of the sideview mirror, waved and stomped his feet and the Lada rocked like a cradle.

END